Hot Brazilian Docs!

Sizzling Brazilian nights with the hottest docs in Latin America!

The hotshot docs of Santa Coração are all top-of-their-class surgeons, and Adam and Sebastian are no exception! But handling a medical emergency is nothing like falling for the two feisty, sexy women who stumble across their paths. Suddenly these Brazilian docs are further out of their depth than they've ever been before!

The **Hot Brazilian Docs!** duet by Tina Beckett is available in September 2017.

Adam's story: *The Doctor's Forbidden Temptation*
Sebastian's story: *From Passion to Pregnancy*

And if you missed them earlier:

Marcos's story: *To Play with Fire*
Lucas's story: *The Dangers of Dating Dr. Carvalho*

Dear Reader,

Best friends! They're wonderful to have. You do everything together: share experiences, celebrate victories and losses…and are adamant about remaining bachelors. Yep, Adam Cordeiro and Sebastian Texeira are childhood buddies, and are both determined to remain unattached. But what happens when one best friend falls for the other best friend's kid sister? Oh, my!

That's exactly what happens to Adam after catching Natália Texeira in her barely-theres. Natália is even less inclined to tie the knot, especially since she's always had a little crush on the hunky Brazilian doc. But when the kindling ignites, it turns into a blaze that nothing can extinguish, not even Sebastian's blatant disapproval.

I loved these two characters. Natália's vulnerability struck a chord with me, and I so wanted to give her the happy ending she deserved.

Thank you for joining Adam and Natália as they struggle to overcome deep emotional issues from their past. And maybe, just maybe, this special couple will decide that love is worth fighting for. I hope you love reading their journey as much as I loved writing it.

Enjoy!

Love,

Tina Beckett

THE DOCTOR'S FORBIDDEN TEMPTATION

TINA BECKETT

HARLEQUIN® MEDICAL ROMANCE™

Recycling programs
for this product may
not exist in your area.

ISBN-13: 978-0-373-21550-8

The Doctor's Forbidden Temptation

First North American Publication 2017

Printed in U.S.A.

www.Harlequin.com

Visit the Author Profile page
at Harlequin.com for more titles.

To my family. As always. I love you!

CHAPTER ONE

THE VIEW WAS SPECTACULAR. At least from where he stood. And not at all what Dr. Adam Cordeiro expected when he opened the door to the exam room.

Instead of eighty-seven-year-old Delfina Benton, who was confined to a wheelchair, the figure in front of him stood on her own two feet. Although all he could see of the person at the moment was a pair of frilly fuchsia panties. And since she was facing away from him and bent over at the waist, trying to force her foot into a pair of black jeans…

Meu Deus do céu.

He glanced at the electronic file in his hand. Room 206. And the placard on the wall beside him read…204. Damn. Wrong room.

Slowly backing away, he was just getting ready to close the door when the figure straightened and then whirled around with a couple of hopped steps until she'd moved far enough to look at him. Her face turned the color of that lacy undergarment. "Adam! What are you trying to do? Give me a heart attack?"

Him? Give *her* a heart attack? He didn't think so.

"You are very lucky it wasn't Sebastian who opened this door."

"I thought I locked it."

One leg was still half-buried in the leg of the jeans, while the other impossibly long limb was completely bare. And sexy.

And…hell, no!

Where was the pale, skinny little girl he'd practically grown up with? Not here, that was for sure.

The woman standing before him was all feminine curves and dark-lashed eyes. And…

Off limits.

Completely off limits. His comment about Sebastian wasn't totally misguided, because if someone happened to come into this room and see them, both he and Natália would have a whole lot of explaining to do. Besides being his best friend, Sebastian Texeira was pretty damn protective of his little sister. With good reason.

"Well, you *didn't* lock it." Realizing the door was still open, he swung it closed, shutting off the view to anyone else who might happen by. It took more strength than he expected, but he somehow managed to pivot to face the door. "You might want to finish what you started."

Except what she'd started was a small fire in the pit of his stomach that was growing bigger by the second. And higher.

Shuffling sounds behind him told Adam that she was taking him at his word. "Thank you for at least turning around."

"There is a staff dressing room, you know."

There was a pause. Then her voice came from behind him. "I was in a hurry. And the floor was practically empty."

Speaking of empty, he was supposed to be seeing a patient right now. "Anyone could have walked in on you, Nata."

Why had he never realized that the shortened version of Natália meant "cream" in Portuguese? And hell if it didn't fit her perfectly right now. A thought that made him brace his hand against the doorjamb.

"Good thing it was you, then."

If she could read his thoughts, she might not be so blasé about saying that. Because while she might view him as an annoying big brother, kind of like she saw Sebastian, Adam wasn't feeling very brotherly right now. Instead, his reaction was something quite…different.

He gritted his teeth. "Are you done yet?"

"Almost."

He tried not to let his brain wander down any more side roads.

This was Natália, Sebastian's baby sister, damn it! But his mind just would not let go of the picture of Nata standing there in a pair of tiny skivvies and a matching bra that barely held her curves at bay. Well, they were even then, because Adam was barely holding some things at bay himself.

He waited a second or two longer, and then she murmured, "It's safe."

It wasn't. Not by a long shot. But that didn't stop him from turning around to face her once again. This time she was fully dressed, her close-fitting jeans topped with a dark green tunic that she'd belted around her waist. Her sleeves came down past her elbows, a habit she'd adopted in her teenage years and still preferred, even on the hottest days of summer. Her hair was a dark disarray of curls that bounced past her shoulders, and he knew from memory that they slid all the way down to the slope of her lower back. She'd always kept those dark locks long.

And he'd never thought of that as sexy before. Until now.

He was in trouble.

"Is Sebastian here?"

Natália glanced around, eyes wide in what had to be fake fear. "I don't know. Did he come sneaking in too?"

"I didn't come sneaking. And you know what I mean."

"No. I really don't." She slung a purple bag over her shoulder, the silver chain matching the color of the belt links. "But I never knew you were the peeping Tom type."

"I'm not." He scowled to cover the fact that he'd done exactly that for the first five seconds after entering the room.

No, you tried to leave as soon as you re-alized what was happening.

And if Natália had been doing something

other than changing? This time it was his face that was growing hot. Not in embarrassment, but in anger. He'd never even seen her hanging out with a man, much less caught her in the act of getting it on with one.

Why would he even care?

Because Sebastian wouldn't approve.

And you, Adam? Would you approve?

Hell and double no. He and his friend had always tag-team protected Nata.

"Well, if you'll excuse me, I have a date."

A date? Adam swallowed. Was that why she had on those sexy undergarments? Because she had always seemed the type to lean more toward utilitarian selections when it came to clothes. Or was he just remembering Nata as a kid and forgetting that she was now a grown woman?

She had a date.

Well, good for her. Adam might not have found happiness at the altar of so-called love and matrimony, but that didn't mean that someone else couldn't find a partner who would honor their vows.

Or at least not cheat on him with someone from the same hospital.

Priscilla had remarried almost before the ink had dried on the divorce decree.

Bile washed into his gut. If someone tried to do that to Natália after everything she'd been through, he would put a fist down their throat.

"Adam?"

His gaze jerked to her face to note that her head was tilted and she was staring at him as if he'd grown horns. "Sorry, did you say something?"

"I was asking if you were going to keep blocking that door." She tugged her left sleeve down just a little bit lower. He'd always hated it when she did that.

Despite her veiled request, he didn't move right away. And he almost didn't move at all. He wanted to know where she was going in all that pink lace. "So you have a date, do you? Does Sebastian know?"

"Yep and no. My plans for tonight are none of my brother's business." The smile she threw him was one he recognized all too well. Full of mischief and laughter, it said she wasn't about to tell him what he wanted to know. Instead she arched her brows in a very feminine move that Adam would have never pictured her doing. Before panty-gate, anyway.

Panty-gate? Oh, brother. He rolled his

eyes and stepped to the side, gripping the door handle and pulling the door open in one swift move designed to let her out so that he could finish his day and see his last patient. And try not to think about what else he had seen or what Natália was going to do that she didn't want her brother to know about. In the meantime, he was going to mind his own business and forget—or at least try to forget—that this unfortunate encounter had ever happened.

Natália Texeira swished down the hallway, trying to look a lot more confident than she felt. In reality, her legs were shaking and her heart was pounding. A date? Well, that was a great line.

Not so great was the look of shock on his face. Did he think she couldn't get one? Well, he could just go and...

Better not to even think that. Because while he might have been surprised about her so-called date night, his reaction to seeing her undressed had been totally masculine.

And totally hot.

She'd dreamed about him looking at her like that for most of her teenaged and young adult years. But since he was six years older than she was, he'd always thought of her as a little kid. Those days were long gone. They were both adults now. He'd been married and divorced. They'd moved past childhood infatuations.

Not that Adam had ever had a crush on her.

She wanted to look behind her. Was dying to know if he was still staring at her. There'd been something in those deep brown eyes that had made her insides sizzle. Of course she'd kept her scarred arm facing away from him, although she had no idea why. He had to have seen it at some point over the years. More than once, despite all her efforts to keep it hidden.

"Nata? Did you forget something?"

His voice sounded from right behind her. Not only was he looking. He'd followed her. She couldn't imagine what he was talking about. Heart in her throat, she spun around to face him.

In his hand he held something brown and shiny and… Her barrette.

The tiny zing of anticipation died a hard death. Ugh. What had she thought he was going to say? That she'd forgotten to kiss him goodbye? Not in this lifetime.

"Thanks." She forced a smile, hoping it was bright and cheery. She gave her sleeve a tug and then held out her hand for her errant hair ornament. In her haste to get away from him, she hadn't realized she'd left her hair down.

"Why do you keep doing that?"

She blinked. "Doing what?"

"Pulling at your sleeve. Is your arm hurting you?" His brows puckered in… Concern. *Oh, God, no. Not again.*

Her smile disappeared. "No. This shirt is just snug."

Liar. Her top was a stretchy, flowy material. The opposite of snug.

"When was the last time you had it checked?"

"Are you kidding me, Adam?" This time it wasn't anticipation that tingled up her back until it hit the base of her skull but raw anger. "I'm a doctor. I think I would know if my prosthesis was giving me trouble."

His wince was unmistakable at her bald words. Well, what she'd said was true. Her prosthetic device might not be visible to the world, but it was there just the same. And for him to ask her about it after the encounter they'd just had was almost unbearable. So much for feeling sexy and confident. He'd just transported her back to when she was sixteen and woken up in a hospital bed with seven inches of her left humerus gone, replaced by a shaft of metal. She found herself bending her elbow, a subconscious response to thinking about the osteosarcoma that had almost taken her arm. If she'd never gotten sick, her life would be very different now.

And maybe Adam would have looked at her through different eyes.

But it was what it was.

"I'm sorry."

The man actually looked penitent, something she couldn't normally say about the handsome orthopedic surgeon. He'd had a reputation as a playboy back in high school, college and for most of med school. All that had changed when he'd gotten married and then divorced a couple of years later. Women still threw themselves at him, but from all accounts those advances were ignored with a quick smile as he went on his way.

Except the way he'd looked at her in that exam room… If she'd wrapped her arms around his neck would he have rebuffed her?

Um, yes, if this conversation was anything to go by. And she would be mortified to have him set her aside like a child. She wasn't a child. And she was going to show him that once and for all.

Only she had no idea how. Or why.

Up went her chin. "You and my brother need to get it through your thick skulls that I do not need protecting. I'm a big girl with big girl panties, and I've been wearing them for quite some time."

"So I've seen." The words were muttered in a low pained tone. At first she thought she'd misunderstood him, but since he was now avoiding her eyes like the plague, she was pretty sure she'd heard him correctly.

Well, then. Maybe she hadn't been wrong about his adult male reaction after all. "That's what you get for walking in on someone—"

"In an unlocked exam room. What if I'd been the hospital administrator?"

"You weren't. Karma wouldn't do that to me."

At least she hoped not. She tried to be nice to those around her. Except when a certain overprotective brother and his hunky cohort started to meddle in her affairs.

Not that she had any affairs worth meddling in.

"Oh, I think karma has a pretty twisted sense of justice."

Was he talking about his divorce? She'd heard his ex-wife had not only married another doctor but she'd gotten a hefty settlement during the divorce trial. Due to some ridiculous lie about how he withheld himself from her emotionally after she'd told him she didn't want children.

Adam was no cold fish. And surely his wife had known how much he wanted a large family. Natália remembered him always talking about wanting lots and lots of kids. Of course, he would tweak her nose as he said it, adding something along the lines of hoping all his little girls were as cute as she was. Only that was never going to happen. Not now. And unlike his ex-wife, it wasn't because Natália didn't want children. "Maybe it does, since you happened to be the one who caught me. Someone who is practically family."

The dig was meant to get a reaction out of him, but she was sorely disappointed. He merely nodded.

She flexed her elbow again, then stopped

mid-movement when his eyes followed the gesture. "It's fine. Just a bad habit."

Kind of like her crush on Adam had been. A bad habit that she'd had the hardest time breaking. But she had. Finally.

Right?

Absolutely. Maybe karma really did have a twisted sense of justice. She couldn't give him what he wanted. In more ways than one.

"If you're sure," he said.

"I am."

He glanced at her face, lingering there for what seemed like an eternity before his gaze brushed down her nose...across her lips. She swallowed, then his index finger came up and tapped under her chin. "I like your hair down, by the way. I don't think I've seen it that way in...well, a long time."

Her mouth popped open, but before her sluggish brain could even think of a response he'd dropped his hand to his side with a lopsided smile. "I'd better go. I have a patient to recheck before I clock out. And you evidently have a hot date."

That's right. She was supposed to be going out on a date with someone besides a bowl of yakisoba from a nearby takeout joint. If her food was hot, it counted, right? Why had she ever concocted that lie? Maybe because she'd been so flustered to have been caught there in her underwear by the very man she'd fantasized about for so many years. "Yep. I'd better go and get ready then."

He started to say something, and then gave his head a brief shake. He took a step or two in the opposite direction and then threw a single line over his shoulder without looking back. "Call me when you get home from your date."

What? Oh, no!

She would be home in a half-hour. Forty-five minutes, tops. And then she would have to come up with a plausible reason why her "date" hadn't lasted longer than it had. She could ignore his order. And have him call Sebastian and very possibly the police?

Not if she could help it. A slow smile curved her lips. That was fine. She'd call him. But she'd wait a couple of hours and make him sweat a little.

He rounded the corner, leaving her standing alone in the hallway with nothing more than her thoughts—which were now running wild with all sorts of possibilities.

But one thing she did know. When she finally put that call through, she was going to have a tale to tell that beat all tales. Of being wined and dined long into the night. She could pick up a bottle of wine with her takeout and watch a romantic movie. So it wouldn't be a total lie. Right?

And he would stay on the other end of that line and listen to the whole darned thing. After that, it was doubtful that Adam Cordeiro would ever try to play big brother to her again.

She was stranded.

Dammit. She turned the key in the ignition of her small car again, only to hear the same ominous click she'd heard for the last five minutes. She'd tried to call three of her girlfriends, including Maggie, but so far two of them had gone to voicemail. The other was working the graveyard shift and Natália hadn't had the heart to ask her to leave the nurses' station right after she'd gotten to work.

She could call Sebastian. And have him give her a lecture about having her car serviced regularly? She tried to remember when the last time had been. But life was so busy with all these hot dates and everything…

She rolled her eyes. Natália had had one serious relationship in her life. And in reality she was too self-conscious about her scar and the questions that would invariably come up. Plus the fact that her chemo treatments meant she could develop lymphoma at some point in her life. And, really, how did one bring up subjects like that with someone you were just getting to know? And yet to not talk about the realities she faced seemed dishonest somehow. To let someone fall in love with her and then suddenly spring it on him: "Hey, I had cancer. And chemo. And a complicated surgery that included having most of my arm bone removed. Oh, and by the way, I'm sterile and might not live to a ripe old age."

Her lungs went tight all of a sudden at the thought of not ever having a baby. *Dammit, Nata, you hold babies every single day.*

But it wasn't the same. She sighed in exasperation.

So, yeah, she never could figure out how to deal with any of that so she just did the next best thing. She didn't date. Or at least she rarely dated. Her boyfriend hadn't even lasted long enough for her to think about The Talk. Maybe because she'd been an uptight neurotic mess the whole time they'd dated. Undressing in the dark had been a huge turnoff for him, and she hadn't wanted him to see her scars so that she didn't have to go into explanations… And, well, it had just been too exhausting to keep up the act.

It was easier just to deal with eating take-out and sleeping alone.

She was going to have to do what she'd vowed not to do. But at least she had the great story she swore she'd have before she talked to him—she had her bottle of wine right next to her. Ugh! She could just catch one of the many buses that came through the area, but in São Paulo, leaving a car un-attended was just asking to have it stolen. Or at least stripped down to almost nothing.

Kind of like she'd been in that exam room.

That got a smile out of her.

He *had* told her to call him, right? And she *had* wanted to make it uncomfortable for him, hadn't she? Well, what could be more uncomfortable than having to come and give her a ride back to her apartment—after call-ing for a tow truck to have her car trans-ported to her place, at least until she could find a service station that had time to fix it.

Securing the carton of yakisoba behind

her purse on the seat so it wouldn't dump out all over her floorboards, she fished out her cellphone. She didn't bother wondering if his number had changed since the last time she'd called him, because she was pretty sure it hadn't. Adam had had the same phone number for the last several years. He didn't deal well with change.

So his divorce had probably not been the easiest thing for him to deal with. But he'd survived. Just like she'd survived a life-changing illness. His ex had been bad news. In Natália's book he was much better off without her.

She took one deep breath and then two, her lips moving as she went through the story she was going to give him when he answered the phone. Then she found his number in her list of contacts and hit the dial button. The phone rang. And rang. And rang again before clicking to voicemail. Natália ground her teeth. Okay, so maybe Adam wouldn't get the satisfaction of rescuing her after all. There was no choice. She had to call Sebastian. Just as she punched in the first two numbers, the cellphone began to ring. She glanced at the screen.

Adam.

Only now she was all frazzled, the planned words swept away.

"Hello?"

"Hi, Adam, it's me, Natália."

"I know who it is. Sorry, I was in the shower and didn't hear the phone right away."

The image of Adam standing on a bath-mat with water streaming down his chest was something that made her brain freeze even further. "I know I said I'd call you when I got home, but I'm…um…kind of stranded."

"Stranded? What do you mean, stranded?" There was silence for a second or two, then his voice came back. "*Meu Deus do céu.* I want a name, Nata."

The low quiet tone held a wealth of menace. How humiliating was this? But she'd called the man. She could hardly pretend she hadn't said the words. "I'm at the yakisoba place down in Santo Amaro."

"I'll be there in a few minutes. But I'm still waiting for a name."

She gulped. "Okay. Palácio de Yakisoba."

"Not the name of the restaurant. The name of your date."

The name of her…

Deus!

That's right, where was that story you thought up?

Not in her head, that was for sure. She did not want to admit that she didn't have a date after all. For some reason she thought he would be far too pleased with that news. And the last thing she needed was for Adam to turn into Sebastian and go all big brother on her. She didn't need two of them. So she decided to hedge.

"It doesn't matter. I just need to be jumped."

Another pause. Longer this time. "Jumped?"

"Yes."

"I don't understand."

Did she have to spell it out? "My car died at the takeout place. I think it's the battery."

A low chuckle came through her phone. "I see. For some reason I thought jumped meant…"

"You thought it meant what?" Natália was thoroughly confused.

"Never mind. So you were the designated driver this evening?"

Well, since she'd designated herself to drive to the restaurant, this question she could answer fairly truthfully. "Yes, yes, I was. It didn't work out quite like I was hoping."

"I'm glad he didn't just leave you without transportation. Not that I approve of him leaving you there with a car that is *quebrado*. Did he find another way home?"

She gulped. "There is definitely something wrong with that picture, isn't there?" Mainly because it wasn't true. Not at all.

"Don't worry, Nata. I will be there in fifteen minutes. Don't go anywhere."

Exactly where was she supposed to go? Her car was stuck here and so was she. "Please don't say anything to Sebastian about this."

"Your brother has a right to know."

"Um, not really. I'm a grown-up, remember?"

"Then you should be grown-up enough to tell him yourself."

Her brother would freak out if he thought some man had abandoned her at a restaurant. She was going to have to tell Adam the truth, dammit. But it could wait until just before she closed the door of her car and left the parking lot. She didn't want to have to endure the expression on his face. Or listen to some kind of quippy comment. Yes, that would be the best route. "Don't worry. I'll let my brother know you turned into my knight in shining armor."

A low dark sound tickled her ear. "I'm no knight, Nata. Remember that. I'll see you soon."

With that he was gone, and she was left standing next to her useless car with an even more useless sense of longing. Why could Adam never see her as an adult?

Maybe because they'd grown up together. Maybe because she had been someone he'd had to be careful around because of her cancer. Whatever it was, he had never seen her as an equal. Even after coming back to Brazil after furthering his training in orthopedic surgery in the United States. That had been after his marriage had taken a wrong turn.

If anything, Adam was more cynical and guarded now than he'd been as a young adult. Who could blame him? His wife had cheated. None of it could have been easy for him.

Shaking her head, she opened the door to her car and got back in. If she could just get the darned thing started, she wouldn't have to face him at all. Her momentary thrill at having gotten a reaction out of him in that exam room had changed to flat-out embarrassment. She'd been mistaken about the expression on his face. She had to be. Her conversation a moment ago confirmed that.

She turned the key in the ignition and heard the same sluggish growl the vehicle had given for the last half-hour. Something was definitely wrong with it.

Another car pulled up beside her. It wasn't Adam, and the young man seated in the passenger seat made her slightly uneasy. Dark hair and hard eyes surveyed what he could see of her, from her hands clenching the steering wheel to the window that was half-open to let in a little cool air. Maybe she should have waited in the restaurant rather than sitting around in the open with her car in obvious trouble. This wasn't a particularly dangerous part of São Paulo, but there were always people out there who were willing to take advantage of a vulnerable situation. Her parents had been robbed at gunpoint twice while stopping at night at a traffic light. People had learned to just run the lights if it was late at night, rather than risking a problem.

"Precisa ajuda?"

His words were nice enough, asking if she needed help.

"No, I'm good. I have someone coming. They should be here any minute."

Instead of discouraging the man, his door clicked open and one scrawny leg appeared followed by another as the man stood. "Maybe I should take a look at it."

"No, I really am okay. I think I'll just—"

Her words were cut off when another car pulled up between them, the sleek front bumper coming within inches of the intruder's knees. The man's head turned so fast that strands of his lank hair fell over his forehead as he shouted, *"Oi, cara, quase me atropelou."*

Oh, damn. That was probably the wrong thing to have said to the owner of this particular vehicle, whose occupant emerged, one hand resting on his door, the other on top of his sports car. "You'll get a lot more than run over, if you take one more step toward her."

The driver of the original vehicle called to his buddy, who scowled for a second or two before ducking back inside. The two then peeled out of the parking lot, a cloud of burning rubber filling the air.

Adam slammed the door to his car and crossed the few feet until he was standing next to her little clunker. "If I try the handle to your door, I will find it locked, will I not?"

Her fingers itched to punch the button that would do just that, but he would hear it. "No, because I was just trying to start it one more time before going back into the restaurant. And I have a pretty powerful scream, if you remember."

One side of his mouth lifted, the anger in his eyes dimming. "I do at that. I also remember how you used to like to shriek right in my and Sebastian's ears."

"Only when you were being really mean. Like setting my dollhouse on fire."

His smile widened. "You never liked that dollhouse."

She shrugged. "It didn't matter. Besides, if anyone was going to burn it down, it was going to be me."

Instead, her parents' fighting had burned down her whole childhood. Sebastian's too. She had made the decision that she would not marry someone unless they could be friends outside of the passion. The problem was finding the right balance. It was either friend/friend. Or passion/passion. So far the terms seemed to be mutually exclusive. Maybe she was looking for a unicorn—something that didn't exist.

"You never did, though." His grin faded just a little. "So, now that the excitement is all over, what seems to be wrong with your car?"

"I think it's the battery. Sometimes it acts like it wants to turn over, but other times it just clicks."

"Try it now."

Natália obliged, turning the key and giving it her best shot. She had no better luck now than just before those thugs showed up. "See? Do you think a jump will work?"

"No. I bet it's your starter, which means it will have to be towed to the shop."

She groaned. "I have to work tomorrow, how am I supposed to get there?"

"We do work at the same place."

No. That was not an option. "I can take public transport."

"Have you seen the subways at rush hour?"

"Yes. I used to ride them to school. We all did."

"That should be reason enough for you to want to avoid them." He motioned for her to give him a minute and then held his phone to his ear. Once he started talking, it was obvious he had a mechanic on the other end of the line.

Perfect. This was all she needed. Her day had gone haywire from almost the moment she got up that morning.

He was off the phone within seconds. "I have a friend who's sending a truck. He said he should be able to have it fixed by tomorrow afternoon."

Not soon enough to avoid having to ride into work with Mr. Tall, Dark, and Ridiculous. Why was he taking over and making decisions for her? "What if I had my own mechanic?"

"Do you?"

"Not really." The misery she felt must have shown on her face because he reached down and opened her door. "Come on, Cinderella. We'll leave your keys with the owner of the restaurant and I'll take you home."

"Public transport." But the words came out as a sullen mutter, because she already knew it would do no good to suggest it.

There was nothing to it but to let Adam take her home.

But if she had her way, it was going to be the shortest trip in history.

CHAPTER TWO

"WHY DID YOU tell me you had a date?"

Taking a long pull of the beer Nata had offered him, he leaned back in his chair and studied her. With her hair now piled on top of her head and held with a clip, she had a sheepish look on her face that almost made him laugh. Almost. Because the wave of fury that had churned to life in his gut when he thought she'd been abandoned by some nameless jerk had shocked him. Sebastian would have been mad too. But his anger would have been because Nata was his sister. What was Adam's excuse?

Something he'd better not examine too closely.

"I have no idea. It just kind of came out. I didn't expect my car to break down or for anyone to find out."

"I bet."

Natália glared at him over her glass of wine. They had split the container of take-out food, Natália saying it was the least she could do to repay him for arranging for the tow and bringing her home. He could have refused to share her meal. Probably should have refused.

He'd been feeling out of sorts for most of the day. Sitting across the table from her wasn't helping.

"You and Sebastian have always tried to run herd on me, and I didn't want you taking up where you left off before you…"

She didn't finish the sentence. What had she been about to say? Before he divorced? Before he left for the United States? Before he'd caught her in her "barely theres" in that damned exam room?

"Your brother and I were worried about you, that's all."

"You babied me. From the moment I got my diagnosis. It was irritating."

"If Sebastian had been diagnosed with cancer, what would you have done?"

Her brows puckered for a few seconds. Then she took a deep breath. "I probably would have done some of the same things.

But not to the ridiculous extent that you both went to."

"I'm pretty sure I remember you flipping out when Sebastian broke his arm, threatening to 'flatten' whoever had tripped him in the school hallway that day."

"Someone told me the person did it on purpose."

"See? You were protecting him." He took another drink of his beer. "The same way we both protected you."

Her jaw lifted to a dangerous angle. "We? There's a difference between you and Sebastian. You are not my brother. And I'm not your sister."

She didn't need to tell him that. Not any more. But it stung that she'd just put him firmly in his place…as an outsider. "Maybe not. But I'm your brother's friend."

And that brother was fiercely protective of his sister. He'd never approved of any boy… or man…who'd been attracted to her. It was probably a normal sibling reaction. Adam had always been careful to keep on the right side of that barrier, never allowing even the slightest hint of interest to show in his words or actions. Not that there'd been any interest between him and Sebastian's sister. They were too far apart in age and too close in other ways. And Adam did not have a good track record when it came to relationships.

Like his high school girlfriend? He'd messed up big that time. Or how about his ex-wife?

Not a good track record at all.

Much better to stay friends with Natália than to ruin things forever.

"Yes, well, that doesn't give you a license to criticize my choices."

"Whoa." He held up his hands. "Exactly how did I criticize you?"

"Well, you..." She swirled her drink in her glass. "I'm sure you would have if I'd actually had a date there in the car with me."

That made him chuckle. "Would you have introduced him to me?"

"Absolutely not." She stood up and held out her hand for the empty plate. "Are you finished?"

"Yes, with everything except for this." He held up the Cellophane wrapper that contained a fortune cookie. "We should probably open it and see what it says."

There was only one cookie, since there had only been one order of food. He wasn't even sure why he'd mentioned it, except that he couldn't remember a time he and Nata had shared a meal together. Not without her brother or someone else being there. He was loath to bring the time to an end for some reason. Maybe because she had called him for help, rather than another friend or her brother.

The slight frown she'd carried all evening disappeared. "If it says something about being unlucky in love I'm going to be seriously ticked." Then she stopped. "I'm sorry, Adam, I wasn't directing that at you."

"It's okay." He'd already been unlucky in love, not once but twice. Not much could be worse than what he'd been through on either of those occasions. "There's not much chance of it predicting my future with any accuracy."

He helped her clear the table, carrying the cookie with them into the kitchen.

"You're never planning on getting married again?"

"Nope. Once was more than enough."

"But what about that big family you said you wanted?" Natália didn't look at him, making short work of scraping the plates and setting them into hot soapy water she'd prepared a few seconds earlier. "Not everyone is like Priscilla."

He didn't really want to discuss his ex. Or children. Or hear Nata say he could very well find someone amazing, if he gave women a chance. "Do you want me to make coffee?"

"Yes, please. The grounds are in the cabinet to your left."

"No fancy pod system?"

"I prefer to do things the old-fashioned way. It helps me appreciate it more."

Adam wasn't going to even touch that one. Because he could think of at least one thing that he preferred to do the old-fashioned way as well. And it didn't involve coffee. Instead he got busy measuring out the grounds and filled the machine with water. He'd only had one beer, but somehow his head was a little fuzzy, as if he'd spent the night at the bar. Maybe it was just everything that had happened: the distress call, those thugs at the *yakisoba* place, finding out that she hadn't had a date after all.

Within ten minutes they were in the living room with a tray, two coffees and the lone fortune cookie between them. Natália settled on the couch, and he set the tray on the table and lowered himself beside her.

She picked up her mug and took a deep sip of the contents, wrapping her hands around it and holding it close to her lips. Her eyes shut for a second. "Perfect. Thank you."

"I aim to please."

Those words came out all rough-edged, loaded with a meaning that had nothing to do with coffee. He purposely cleared his throat, to make it seem like that was to blame and not his own damned inner processes that had been running rampant all day.

He picked up the fortune cookie and tossed it in the air, catching it with a flick of his wrist and shoving his open palm toward her. "I think you should do the honors."

It definitely shouldn't be him. Not when he was suddenly aware of every move she made…of every glance she angled toward him. Of those damned panties that he knew lay just beneath her sensible clothing. Down that path was madness and irresponsibility. And self-destruction.

Natália's brown eyes met his for a second and then she set her mug down and plucked the fortune cookie from his palm. Her lips twisted to one side. "Chicken."

Yes. He was. And he was okay with that label. It was better than some of the angry accusations he was currently throwing at himself.

The crinkling of plastic seemed louder than normal. He set his own coffee down as he waited for her to finish opening the package. Then it was in her hand. "We'll split it."

She broke the cookie in two and handed him the half without the little slip of paper sticking out of it. Then, gripping the fortune with her thumb and forefinger, she teased it from its home. Popping her half of the cookie in her mouth, she turned the paper over so she could read it.

Her jaws suddenly stopped chewing, her eyes widening in something akin to horror.

"What?" he asked. "It's not predicting one of our deaths, is it?"

He didn't really think it was, but the color was seeping out of her cheeks. "Do you want me to read it?"

Her mouth went back to working on the food, moving in jerky starts and stops before her throat moved and she swallowed.

Something was bothering her. "What does it say, Nata?"

She licked her lips. "It's stupid. I should just throw it away."

Maybe she should. But now he wanted to know what was on it. What she thought was so terrible that she didn't even want to voice it aloud. It was nonsense, right? Then why was he suddenly worried that his past might be rising up to find him?

"Either read it or give it to me."

"Fine. You want to know what it says? I'll tell you." Her chest heaved as she took a deep breath and then blew it out audibly. "Don't say I didn't warn you."

Her head bent as she leaned closer to whatever was written on that paper. "'Soon you will meet and kiss someone special.'"

The words ricocheted through the room, bouncing around as his head tried to make sense of them. Then they registered, and he laughed in relief. "That's what you were so upset about?"

"Well, I know it's stupid, but it's a little embarrassing, don't you think?"

"No, I don't think." He slid his fingers over the side of her cheek. "I did meet you at that restaurant. And I'm at least a little special, aren't I?"

"Well, of course."

He leaned sideways and kissed her cheek. "See? Painless. That wasn't embarrassing, was it?"

"No, I guess not." She smiled.

"Your turn, since the fortune was for both of us." He presented his cheek to her.

The second she touched her lips to his skin, though, he knew he'd made a huge mistake in asking her to reciprocate. The kiss hit him just beside his mouth, the pressure warm, soft and lingering just a touch too long. Long enough for his hand to slide to the back of her head, his fingers tunneling into her hair. Then, before he could stop himself, his head slowly turned toward the source of that sweet heat until he found it. Leaned in tight.

Instead of her pulling away, he could have sworn the lightest sigh breathed against his mouth. And that was when he kissed her back. Face to face. Mouth to mouth.

It was good. Too good. He tilted his head to the side, the need to fit against her singing through his veins. He captured a hint of the coffee she'd drunk, and the wine, his tongue reaching for more of the same.

He forgot about the meal, the fortune cookie…everything, as the kiss went on far beyond the realm of the words "platonic" and "friend" and into the hazy kingdom where lovers dwelt.

Every moment from this morning until now seemed to have been spiraling toward this event.

A soft sound came from her throat and the fingers in her hair tightened into a fist, whether to tug free or pull her closer, he had no idea. Then her mouth separated from his and she bit the tip of his chin, the sharp sting jerking at regions below his belt, a familiar pulsing beginning to take over his thoughts. If he didn't bring this to a halt now…

Somehow he managed to let go of her hair and place both of his palms on her shoulders, using the momentum to edge her back a few inches. Then a few more.

"Nata…we can't do this." The words didn't seem all that convinced. "Sebastian would kill us."

His friend would approve of him using his name as a weapon. At least in this case.

Brown eyes blinked up at him. "Why does he have to know?"

"If you think he wouldn't find out, you're wrong." He kissed the corner of her mouth, trying to force a playful edge to the act. "Let's not take that fortune too seriously."

Her gaze went from warm to cool in the space of a few milliseconds. "I wasn't taking anything too seriously. But maybe you were."

Hell, maybe he was. Maybe that was behind the need to claw his way back to reality. A reality he wasn't enjoying all that much right now.

"Nope. I just don't want anyone to get the wrong idea."

There was silence for a second or two. "I'm taking it that that person wouldn't be you."

His disastrous youth came to mind. All the more reason not to ruin a good friendship over a stupid impulsive move. Like kissing Natália? "No, it wouldn't be me."

"And you're arrogant enough to think I would fall down and bawl my eyes out if you say you aren't attracted to me?"

No one had said anything about being attracted to her. Obviously he was, although he was smart enough not to let his thoughts stray too far in that direction. At least not often.

He tried to soften his words. "I can't imagine anyone who *wouldn't* be attracted to you, Nata. You're beautiful and kind. Everything a normal man could want."

"You forgot to mention my uncanny ability to see through bullshit."

He had not forgotten that, which was why he'd wanted to end the kiss before she read through it and saw something very different. She'd always been able to read people, even as a teenager. Maybe because of all the medical professionals she'd been through. With a maturity that often far outweighed her years, she had known when someone was trying to placate her or when they were telling the raw, unvarnished truth. Thank God, though, that she hadn't been able to tell how shocked he'd been by his reaction to that kiss. And if he had his way, she never would, since he wasn't likely to repeat his mistake.

"Your brother, unfortunately, tends to see things that aren't there."

"Do you honestly think I am going to go running to him and tell him we sat in my apartment and made out?"

Made out. Hell, the woman didn't know the meaning of that word, because had he gotten that far, Natália would have been flat on her back on the sofa and there would have been a very different outcome. *Graças a Deus* he'd come to his senses in time.

"No…" He dragged a hand through his hair, trying to figure out a way to explain this that didn't get him into even hotter water. "So we'll keep this strictly between us."

Her mouth twisted sideways. "Do you want me to pinkie swear?"

"Not necessary." Besides, he didn't want to touch her again. Standing to his feet, he motioned toward the coffee table. "Can I help you clean up?"

She stood as well. "No, I've got it. I guess I'll see you tomorrow at the hospital."

With that, Adam headed for the nearest escape route: the front door. "Thank you for dinner."

"Thank you for rescuing me."

Adam heard a weird note behind the statement. "You're welcome. My friend texted that he should be able to get to your car sooner than he thought. It may be back by tomorrow morning. I can come by and pick you up for work, if not."

"Thanks, but I've got it."

He frowned. "Call me if it hasn't been delivered. I'll need to check on its progress." He wasn't trying to contradict her or irritate her any more than necessary, but he'd been the one to call the repair shop and have her car towed away. The least he could do was make sure it arrived safely back at her place.

She reached around him and opened the door. "I will. Or I can call Sebastian."

"Do you really think that's a good idea?"

Up went her brows. "Do you really think *this* was a good idea?"

"It wasn't all bad, was it?"

"No. Dinner was great."

Meaning kissing him had not been. He could call her a liar—hell if she hadn't kissed him back—but what would be the point? Maybe it was better for them both to just leave things where they were.

They gave each other a quick goodbye, then Adam stepped through the door and waited until it closed and the deadbolt engaged before heading back to his own car. Yes, putting this behind them was the smartest thing. He could only hope that Natália threw that damned fortune from the cookie into the trash and forgot about tonight…and everything leading up to it.

"We kissed."

Natália said the words in a pseudo-whisper, even though she and her best friend Maggie Pinheiro were alone in the exam room. Married to a family friend, Maggie and Natália had hit it off from the moment they'd met at the couple's wedding four years ago. Maggie, her husband Marcos, Natália and Sebastian all worked at the same hospital, in fact. And now Maggie was pregnant. Very pregnant.

"You kissed who?"

Natália shook her head, suddenly remembering that she hadn't seen Maggie in the two days since she'd had Adam over to her apartment and locked lips with him. Thank God her car had been delivered the morning after, so she hadn't needed to call him and ask him for anything else. It was all too humiliating. Not only having to confess that she didn't have a date but kissing the man like a hungry piranha finding its first good meal after the rains came.

Women loved Adam and the man knew

it. He had to. She saw the looks they gave him in the hospital corridors.

"Adam Cordeiro."

"The orthopedic surgeon?"

Maggie was an American who'd come over to Brazil on a special exchange program and who'd ended up staying after she married Marcos. Although she was fluent in the language, she still had a charming accent and periodically stumbled over an unfamiliar word or phrase.

"Yes."

"Aren't he and Sebastian good friends?"

Natália crinkled her nose. "Yes. We all kind of grew up together."

"I bet that was awkward."

"It was horrible."

Maggie's eyes widened as she sat on the table, waiting for her obstetrician to get there. "The kiss? I always thought Dr. Cordeiro was kind of cute."

"Says the woman who is pregnant with another hottie's baby."

Her friend's hands smoothed over her round belly. "Oh, believe me, I am not looking to swap partners."

"Adam is not my partner."

"I would hope not, if he's a terrible kisser."

Natália's eyes closed for a second before she looked at her friend again in exasperation. "That's the problem. It wasn't a horrible kiss. It was a good kiss."

"I thought you just said it was bad."

This time she laughed. "No. Not the kiss. That was phenomenal. The horrible part was that it was Adam and not someone else."

"You don't like him?"

She dropped into the chair across from the table. "He's like a brother. Well, more like he sees me as an annoying little sister. He only kissed me because the fortune cookie told him to."

"What? Okay, Nata. You have got to slow this train down a little bit. I have no idea what you're talking about."

"Well, I certainly hope not because that would mean everyone else at the hospital knows what happened."

"Including your brother?"

Natália groaned and leaned forward in her chair, rubbing the scar hidden beneath her white lab coat. Images of her teenage years and the way everyone had coddled and protected her came to mind. Including Adam.

"Don't even talk about Sebastian. Adam was more worried about him finding out than anything else." She quickly gave her friend a summary of what had happened between her and Adam, zeroing in on how she had kissed him on the cheek, only to have him suddenly swoop down and cover her mouth with his. It had been...magical. And horrible. And...confusing.

Maggie slid off the table and came to sit on the chair next to hers, making sure her hospital gown was firmly covering her thighs, Natália noticed. Her friend had scars of her own from where she'd self-harmed many years ago. "So, did you want it to be different than it was?"

Did she? Natália had no idea really. Did she want Adam to be attracted to her?

Hadn't he said that any man in his right mind would be? Yes. Which meant he was just giving her a logical excuse for that kiss. Logical, though, meant that he didn't see his reaction to her any differently than his reaction to any woman he found attractive.

So how many women besides his ex-wife had he kissed the same way he had her?

Was she kidding? This was Adam she was talking about.

So that number was way more than she cared to imagine.

"It would be far too complicated between us. He is as irritating and bossy as Sebastian. He doesn't see me as an adult."

Maggie covered her hand with hers. "I don't think that's quite true. If that kiss was anything like you say it was, he definitely sees you as an adult. Even if he doesn't want to admit it."

"You think so?" The question was rhetorical, she didn't really want an answer. Or did she?

"I do." Maggie stood and wiggled her way back onto the exam table. "And if this baby keeps putting off making an appearance, his little brother is going to be all grown up with children of his own."

Natália tensed for a moment before forcing herself to relax again. This was one of her best friends. And if anyone deserved to have a healthy, happy baby, it was her.

"You still have six weeks before your due date."

Her friend groaned. "Do not remind me. I am ready to pop."

With that, the conversation thankfully returned to Maggie's pregnancy and how far behind her friend was in decorating the nursery and making room for the pile of baby clothes she expected to amass at the baby shower Natália was throwing for her. "You can't have the baby before the shower."

"How about as soon as it's over?"

Natália laughed. "Yes. As soon as it's over I will personally drive you to the hospital."

She could only hope that the party and all the preparations leading up to it would help take her mind off of a certain handsome orthopedic surgeon.

Or else she was in big trouble.

CHAPTER THREE

ADAM CAREFULLY WASHED the exposed femur of all visible dirt in preparation for debriding. A motorcycle accident earlier this afternoon had resulted in Katia Machado's bone being forced through her skin and clothing as she slid along a dirt road. As a result, small bits of gravel and red clay had been ground into the wound. The warm, moist atmosphere of his patient's body would provide a haven to all kinds of pathogens, including tetanus. He needed to make sure the injury site and everything inside was pristine by the time he closed her leg back up.

Examining his incision to make sure it was large enough, he began the complex process of undoing all the damage Katia had done to her leg. Kind of like he needed to do with Natália?

Fixing that problem wouldn't be as cut

and dried as the surgery he was now doing. What had come over him? He hadn't drunk that much. Neither had Nata. And yet they'd both acted completely out of character. And he'd behaved almost as irresponsibly as he had when…

He gritted his teeth to stop the flow of recriminations.

"Suction, please." Beads of perspiration gathered on his upper lip in the air pocket beneath his surgical mask, but he didn't stop to blot them, not wanting to further the risk of contamination to the wound.

He and Nata were eventually going to have to sit down and talk this through, or that ill-fated kiss would hang over their friendship and ruin it. He didn't want that to happen. And he had been aware enough to realize that Natália had had a little crush on him when she'd been a teenager. Thank God that stage hadn't lasted long. Then those brown eyes had fixed themselves on someone her own age and off she'd gone.

There's only six years between you, Adam.

It might not seem like a big deal now, but when he had been twenty-three and she'd only been seventeen and still in the midst of her battle with osteosarcoma and the resulting surgery to remove a large section of the bone in her arm, it had been impossible.

It was still impossible, and not because of the age difference. There were a whole lot more factors in play now. And it was just not worth it. Nata knew the happy-go-lucky boy who'd hopped from one girl to another back then. She did not know the cynical, jaded man he'd grown in to.

Or maybe she did.

He could only hope. He wouldn't have been good for her back then. And he certainly wouldn't be good for her now.

As soon as the suction cleared away the blood and fluid that had gathered in the tissues, he used a gloved finger to explore further back, making sure everything was tight and secure, no sign that her bone had ripped through any other tissue. Using a squirt bottle, he rinsed the area again, the loupes he wore magnifying everything and helping him spot anything foreign as the water carried it out.

Too bad those special glasses couldn't help him peer into Nata's head and help him repair what he had messed up. Instead, he was flying blind and every word he'd spoken in her apartment afterwards had seemed to make things worse.

He knew she'd hated the way he and Sebastian had treated her like cracked glass, afraid the slightest knock would cause her to shatter into a thousand pieces. She'd surprised both of them, not only by *not* breaking but powering through her whole ordeal with a lot more grace than he might have done. And she'd come out the other end a beautiful and mostly confident woman. There was still that scar that she kept hidden. Brazilian women liked their clothes and when it was hot, those clothes were designed to help keep them as cool as possible. And Adam had never fully understood why Natália had wanted so desperately to be a neonatologist when she couldn't have children of her own. Or maybe it was because of that.

He avoided that floor of the hospital, because it might not hurt Nata to work there, but it caused a kind of pang in his gut when he thought about her cuddling those babies every single day—especially knowing the awful truth about himself.

Dragging his thoughts back to the job at hand, he inspected his work and made sure everything was as absolutely sterile as he could and then motioned to his assistant. "Let's line up the bone, so I can set the pins." Danielle moved to the knee, while Adam stayed where he was, handing his instruments to one of the nurses. Tugging the bones in opposite directions, they were able to maneuver them so the broken ends joined back together. Then, with Danielle keeping everything in place, he quickly drilled the pins into the bones.

He knew where he'd gone wrong with Nata. He just didn't know how to rectify his mistake. Not without insulting her. Or, worse, hurting her feelings.

Hell, what if they'd spent the night together? He'd have to do something a whole lot stronger than hurt her feelings if that was the case.

Yeah, things could definitely be worse than they were. The only thing to do was finish this surgery and find Natália. Then together they could come up with a game plan on how to handle this whole thing. Either that or he'd better turn tail and run for the next big city. And if there was one thing Adam didn't do, it was run.

* * *

Propping the tiny form up on her shoulder, she stared at the familiar figure standing outside the viewing area. Adam? Here in the neonatal intensive care unit?

She could count on one hand the number of times he'd been down here. Actually, on two fingers. He'd come to visit her floor exactly twice. She'd been up to Orthopedics lots of times. She had friends up there. She guessed Adam didn't have any friends in her department. Except for her, that was.

Unless they were no longer friends.

Her heart shot down her throat, lodging somewhere in her abdomen. Was he here to tell her that he wanted nothing to do with her?

He motioned at the interior of the room in an unspoken question. *Can I come in?*

More than anything she wanted to shake her head and tell him there was no trespassing. Not on her turf and not in her heart. But she also wanted to know what he wanted.

She mouthed a single word, "Yes."

Her palm smoothed over the tiny back of the preemie, letting the almost weightless form anchor her in place. Coward that she was, the baby also formed a shield that she could keep between her and Adam. Not that she had any reason to fear he would jump her in the preemie unit. Or anywhere else, for that matter. He'd made that perfectly clear.

She held up fingers one at a time to give him the key code that would let him into the locked area, a new security feature to prevent any unauthorized person from gaining access to the babies or any of the supplies. Three weeks ago they'd had an angry family member try to abduct one of the babies. Luckily a nurse had seen something suspicious and called Security. The person had been apprehended as the baby slept on unaware. No one had been harmed, but the hospital had made some changes to prevent anything like that from happening again.

Maybe she could do the same with her heart: install a code that would prevent intruders from gaining access to it.

Like Adam?

That man had probably decoded lots of those locks, from what she'd seen.

Within a minute, he had made it past the door and stood over her. "I haven't been down here in ages."

Ages was an understatement. And she

had no idea what brought him all the way over here now. But she had a feeling she wasn't going to like whatever it was. And if the damn man apologized, she was going to blow a fuse. "So why today?"

"I'm sorry I—"

She held up a hand. "*Meu Deus*. Don't even."

"Don't even what?"

"Don't you dare apologize."

Up went one side of that firm mouth, a crease in his cheek making itself known. "I was going to apologize for interrupting your work, but if it irritates you that much, I'll have to say I'm sorry more often."

She wasn't sure what to say to that. Her hand stopped its stroking motions for a second, until the baby shifted, reminding Natália of her presence. She feathered her fingers down the tiny back and patted her gently. This was actually the nurse's job, but Natália came down here every chance she got to cuddle these tiny ones. Wishing for something that would never be?

Maybe. But it brought her comfort in some unfathomable way.

"Speechless?"

"Worried is more like it. Is everything

okay?" A sudden thought hit her. "Sebastian?"

Adam went over to the far wall and pulled up a second rocking chair, moving it over to where she was sitting. "He's fine, as far as I know. But I did come here to talk to you about him."

All of a sudden he wouldn't meet her eyes.

"I don't understand."

"I don't think he would be happy with either of us about what…happened. I want to figure out how to present a united front."

"United? I thought we already did that. I'm not going to tattle on you, Adam, if that's what you're worried about. We're not children. Not any more."

The days of telling on each other were long gone.

"I know we're not. I just don't want to put you in an awkward situation. Or make you feel like you have to lie to keep from saying anything." His glance went from her to the baby and something dark slipped through his eyes before disappearing. "Would you mind putting her down for a minute?"

"Is she making you nervous?" She'd never thought of Adam as not liking babies, but he seemed distinctly uncomfortable by the newborn's presence. Or maybe that was a result of the whole situation. Whatever it was, Natália obliged, getting up and carefully placing the baby back in her environmentally controlled unit. "Better?"

"Yes, thanks."

Normally, on her break she would have gone from patient to patient, trying to give them some contact that didn't involve machines, but it could wait until she wasn't staring at the face of a man she'd practically devoured on her couch. She went back to her seat, her hands clasped in her lap, and looked him in the eyes. "Is this visit really about me, or is it about you trying to stay on good terms with my brother?"

"Maybe a little bit of both. I made a mistake. I'm trying to undo it."

There it was. The second worst thing he could have said—an apology being first on that list. Her reply stung as it made its way past her lips. "It was a mistake we *both* made. We've already agreed it's never happening again. There is absolutely no reason for Sebastian to even ask about it. Unless you give him a reason to."

"I wasn't planning on it."

"Then there you go. It's all good."

Adam's hand went to the arm of her rocking chair. "Is it? All good, I mean?"

"Between us?" Her heart ached. Because he'd been worried about her having to lie to Sebastian, when it was really Adam she'd be lying to. "Yes. It's all good."

"I'm glad, because if anything came between us…" His index finger reached over and stroked the sleeve of her lab coat, sending a shiver down her spine. "Well, I wouldn't be happy."

"That makes two of us." And there it was, the unvarnished truth. Had she really been naive enough at one time to think that she could have a fling or date with him without any repercussions? Without it changing their relationship? Maybe she had back then, but she was older and wiser now. She wasn't like Adam, able to sleep with woman after woman and then go on as if nothing had ever happened. If they had gone past kissing, it would change everything. For her at least. So she had to make sure it didn't.

She tried to reassure him the best she could. "It'll be okay, Adam. It was just a tiny blip on the radar."

Something pounded on the glass outside,

making her jump, while Adam cursed under his breath.

When she looked up, the person they'd just been talking about was standing outside, staring in at them. She hurriedly glanced toward Adam to find a muscle in his jaw working. "What's he doing here?"

"I have no idea." She held up a finger to tell her brother she'd be there in a minute. "You don't have plans with him?"

"No."

"Nossa." Surely he couldn't have figured anything out. Unless her brother and Adam used the same mechanic, but she knew Adam well enough to know that he'd been discreet. "What do you want to do?"

"You might start by letting him in." He smiled at her, but there was a tension behind the expression that she didn't like. "The longer we sit here, the guiltier we look."

"We are guilty," she muttered half to herself. But she got up from her chair and went over to the door, Adam following her. Signaling to the nurse at the main desk to come and take her place, they exited the glassed-in room.

As soon as they got out the door, Sebastian grinned at his friend. "Having a baby, Adam?"

Heat poured into Natália's face, and she knew herself well enough to know that she was beet red.

"Of course not. Why would you think that?" Adam's voice was tight. Angry-sounding, actually.

"Because you're sitting in the nursery."

"That doesn't mean I'm going to start a family anytime soon. When I do, it will be something *both* parties agree to."

Natália cringed. Was Adam sending her a veiled hint? Surely he remembered that she couldn't have children. Or maybe he was making sure—in front of a witness—that she knew he wasn't interested in her in that way. Well, he could have saved himself the trouble.

Sebastian held up his hands. "Whoa. I was kidding, *cara*. I actually came to ask for a consult on a patient who's due to arrive in the next hour or so from Rio Grande do Sul." Her brother glanced her way before giving her a second—harder—look. "Are you okay? You look a little sunburned or something. What are you two doing sitting in the nursery, anyway?"

Her brain went into overdrive, words tumbling over themselves. "My car broke down a couple of days ago, and Adam helped me out. He was just checking to see if the shop got my vehicle back to me without any problems."

"Why didn't you call me?"

"I tried." *Graças a Deus* that she'd started to dial his number when Adam hadn't answered right away.

He seemed to think for a moment. "I was... Wait a minute, where the hell was I?"

"I don't know. I wasn't there." She plastered a smile on her face, although she found nothing even remotely amusing about the situation.

"So is your car okay?"

"Yep, it was the starter, just like Adam thought it was. It's as good as new." She didn't tell him about the two *moleques* that had harassed her or how Adam had arrived just in the nick of time. Or about the fortune cookie. Or that damned kiss.

Her brother rubbed the back of his neck. "Thanks for stepping in and helping her out, Adam."

"It wasn't a problem."

She was thankful he didn't expand on that answer.

"What do I owe you?"

That made her scowl. "You don't owe him anything. It was my car, I'll take care of it." She wasn't going to admit that she had already tried to get Adam to take money for the tow and repairs, and he'd refused. If anything would make Sebastian take a closer look, it was that. There had been so much turmoil in their household that the siblings had quickly learned to take care of any problems between the two of them, never asking for help. Since Sebastian was the same age as Adam, he'd gotten a job long before she had, helping her buy clothes and other necessities. She'd always meant to do the same for her brother now that they were adults, but he wouldn't hear of it. Of course.

"Don't get all huffy, Nata. I was just trying to help."

"I know, and thank you." She knew he was anxious to get back to work, but she was nervous about him and Adam going off together. He could say something he shouldn't. "Is there anything else?"

Sebastian eyed her again, a slight frown

between his brows. "Why are you so grouchy all of a sudden?"

"I'm not. It's just been kind of a crazy day."

And not just today. But the craziness from her apartment was spilling over into her job now. Not good.

Adam broke in, "What did you need help with, anyway?"

"I have a *gaúcho* coming in who was thrown from his horse and fractured his leg. Only he swore that something in his leg snapped first and caused the fall rather than the other way around."

"So why are you handling it, instead of Orthopedics?"

Sebastian was an oncologist, so she could see why Adam was asking.

"Because the cowboy was right. They did an MRI to see how much damage the fracture caused and found…a problem."

Natália stiffened at the way her brother had punched out those words. As if he'd been about to say something and then changed his mind at the last second. "A problem. As in a growth?"

"Yes. Possibly." He glanced her way. "That's why he's headed up here."

Adam's soft curse said it all. He knew exactly what she'd been thinking. Because he was thinking the very same thing.

"How bad is it?" she asked.

"Bad. He might lose the leg, if it's what I think it is."

"Osteosarcoma?"

Natália was living proof of how that word could change the course of someone's life. She'd been lucky. They'd been able to do a limb-salvaging surgery that landed her with an internal prosthesis rather than an amputation. It had still rocked the foundation of her world—the chemo, the surgeries, and the fear that it would come back. The fact that she could never give birth to children. Ever. No one had thought to harvest eggs from her when her cancer had first been discovered, and the poison they'd had to give her to save her had killed off the potential for babies.

Her fingers went to her sleeve where the scar was hidden before realizing both Sebastian and Adam were staring at her.

"Are you okay, *lindinha*?" her brother asked.

"I'm fine." Why did she always end up having to say that to everyone? "Can they do the same surgery I had?"

Adam answered. "It depends on the size of the tumor and what shape his leg is in. If the blood supply to the bone below the break has been compromised or damaged by the trauma of the fall, it may not be possible."

Her throat tightened. "Try. Please." She knew exactly how proud the *gaúchos* from that region were. Their livelihood depended on them being strong and robust. A cowboy without a leg... Well, he would adapt. He would have to, if it came down to that, but what if the leg could be saved? Shouldn't they at least consider the option?

"I'll look at him, Nata, but I can't promise anything." Adam hesitated. "You know the conditions have to be just right for it to work."

She was well aware that the stars had aligned in her favor, although she hadn't felt quite so lucky at the time.

"It's why I came up to find him, sis. I want to do everything possible to save the leg. From what I've heard, the man gave the other hospital a very hard time, threatening to walk away if they even considered taking it." He sighed. "It's not going to heal. The break probably happened because the tumor ate through the bone until it could no longer stand up to the day-to-day stress that riding put on it."

"They're sending him here because the country knows that Hospital Santa Coração is the best there is," she said. "It's up to you guys to prove them right."

Her brother grinned. "Well, thanks for not putting any pressure on us."

"Can I see him?"

He shook his head. "I don't think that's a good idea. At least not now. I want to take this slowly. Give him a chance to process things without…"

"Without seeing a living example of what he'll soon be going through?"

"That's not what I was going to say."

Maybe sensing that things between Natália and her brother were about to grow heated, Adam took a step forward. "I want to examine him before anyone jumps to conclusions. Test results have been wrong before. I don't want to alarm him unnecessarily if it turns out that he doesn't have a tumor after all but a simple break."

There was no way Sebastian would have come looking for Adam unless he was pretty sure the man had osteosarcoma. But maybe the orthopedic surgeon was right. It wouldn't do any good to alarm the patient or, on the other hand, hand out hope, if it wasn't going to be possible to do the surgery. And seeing her with an arm that was still attached to her body might do just that.

"Okay." She straightened her limb as far as she could, needing to assure herself that everything was still okay. "But will you keep me updated on how he's doing?"

Sebastian dropped a hand on her shoulder. "Are you sure you want to know?"

"If something good can come out of my own experience then, yes, I want to know."

She had joined a support group with her brother's help once her own surgery was completed, since she didn't want to place any more stress on her parents' already strained relationship. Sebastian had shielded her as best he could from what was going on, but Natália had been no fool.

"Okay, how about if I let you know once I've examined him and Adam has had a chance to weigh in? Whether or not you can help will depend on what we both think is in the best interests of the patient."

"I understand. But you'll let me know."

"Yes. We will."

So much for avoiding Adam, like she'd

toyed with. Here she was offering to help on one of their cases. But she couldn't let her own petty fears stop her from helping someone else. If this *gaúcho* found himself in the same situation that she'd once been in, she would swallow her fears and push ahead. Just like she'd had to do as her own treatment progressed. She'd never felt totally alone because she'd had Adam and Sebastian to talk to.

Maybe this cowboy had his own support system. It was very possible that he wouldn't need her at all. But if he did, Natália wanted to make sure he had someone. And if she had to work beside Adam to do that, then she would.

No matter how hard it was.

Or how emotionally dangerous it turned out to be.

CHAPTER FOUR

"Of course I can be there. Did you say thirty minutes?"

A week and a half after she'd first learned about the *gaúcho* with the broken femur, she found herself speaking to Adam on the phone. She did her best not to think about how their fortune cookie had predicted they would kiss or how it had come true.

"I can try to get the patient to reschedule the appointment if it's a problem."

Okay, so he didn't sound very happy to have her on the line. Maybe Sebastian had put him up to it.

"No, I'll be able to take off." She hesitated. "Is he resisting having surgery?"

"Worse. He's refusing treatment of any kind, which is why I think he's calling the team in. Sebastian tried to talk to him about using chemo to shrink the tumor, and that's when he demanded to see everyone involved with his treatment."

Her heart caught in her chest. She remembered those days far too well. Even though she was a teenager when her tumor had been discovered, she'd freaked out, saying she'd rather die than lose her arm.

And thank God she hadn't thought about babies back then, or she might have refused treatment as well. "He'll change his mind. Sometimes people just need time to process things."

"I don't know. He's pretty proud."

"But if you and Sebastian talk to him, he'll see how important this is." Even with the infertility issue, she was very glad to be alive.

There was a sigh on the other end of the phone. "We've both tried. So far he's not budging."

"I'll be there in thirty minutes." What did she think she could do that his treatment team couldn't? She wasn't sure. She only knew that if she didn't try, she would never forgive herself.

"Thank you, Nata."

The warmth in his tone was unmistakable. Where at first he'd seemed reluctant, brusque even about her getting involved, he now sounded grateful.

"You're welcome. I'll see you in a little while."

With that she hung up the phone, staring at it for a second as if she wasn't sure the exchange had really happened. But it had.

She hurried through the remainder of the time, finishing up a few little details, and then signed out and told her colleagues where she was going. It had been a quiet shift on the NICU ward.

When she arrived in the oncology ward, she found Sebastian waiting for her. "Adam told me he'd called you. I wish he'd asked me first."

So it wasn't Sebastian who'd asked for her. "Why, so you could have told me not to come?"

"No, but I hate the memories it's going to drag up for you." Her brother paused, stretching one arm behind his back until his shoulder joint made an audible pop— something he habitually did to relieve an old high school *futebol* injury. "What's going on between you and Adam, anyway? Ever since your car broke down, he's been acting strangely."

He had? "Nothing. Why?"

"He's been almost as grouchy as you. Did you two have a fight or something on your way home?"

Relief swept through her. She was afraid he was going to suspect something far less innocent than a quarrel. "No. But maybe you should ask him and not me. It's probably something work related."

"I did ask him. He told me to mind my own business."

Relief turned to shock. "What?"

"Exactly."

"I'm sure it has nothing to do with me." She chanced a quick grin. "And maybe you *should* mind your own business, did you ever think of that?"

Her brother's eyebrows cranked skyward. "Spoken by someone who is waiting to talk to a complete stranger about his business."

"There were people who did the same for me when Mom and Dad couldn't. Or wouldn't. They wanted to pretend none of it was happening." And it was true. They'd avoided talking to her about her disease whenever possible. Except for behind closed doors when there had been raised voices, her dad telling her mom something so horrible that Natália had had difficulty processing it at the time. Even this many years afterwards, he had no idea that she'd overheard him. But when Natália had drawn in on herself, a teacher at school had coaxed her to confide about her cancer and her feelings about it. That woman had been instrumental in changing her attitude, which had been fatalistic at best—suicidal at worst. Without her intervention the outcome might not have been nearly as good.

"I'm sorry you had to live through any of that, Nata. I just don't want Adam to be harassing you into helping with patients every time you turn around."

"He didn't harass me. And this is the first time he's ever asked me to step in on a case. Are you seriously against me being here?"

"No," he admitted with a sheepish smile. "It could help. I just don't want to see you put through the wringer emotionally."

Overprotective to the end. Just like he always was. Only Natália was sick and tired of him and Adam still treating her with kid gloves. She had lived through hell, yes. But it had made her stronger, not weaker.

"I want to be here, Sebastian. If I didn't,

I wouldn't have agreed." She hesitated. "Where is Adam, anyway?"

"He's already in with the patient."

"And the rest of the team?"

"They're waiting on us to call them. Adam wants to give you a chance to talk to the man first."

She nodded. "Then let's get to it, shall we?" She fidgeted with the left sleeve of her light sweater, making sure she hadn't rolled it up too high.

Sebastian pushed the door open and waited for her to walk through it.

Her eyes sought out Adam before flitting to a middle-aged man lying on the exam table. "Hello."

Lean and wiry with a shock of salt and pepper hair and a couple days' worth of whiskers on his jaw, there was a brittleness to him that worried her. He wasn't used to being sick, that much was obvious, and from the stiff set of his mouth he was in considerable pain. His leg was encased in white *gesso*, the cast probably just there to keep the bones from shifting rather than to promote healing. Because there would be no healing of this leg. Not in the traditional sense.

Adam moved to stand beside her. "Mr. Moreira, this is Dr. Texeira. She's Dr. Sebastian Texeira's sister."

"Sister and brother, huh? They let you work on the same patients?" The man's grizzled chin barely moved as he spoke. "That seems kind of suspicious, if you ask me."

Natália spoke up. "I'm not part of your team, but Adam—Dr. Cordeiro—asked me to come up and visit with you."

"Why?"

"Because I know first-hand what you're going through." She kept her voice soft, but made sure there was no trace of pity in it.

"Really?" He cocked his head and studied her with hard eyes. "I don't see how that's possible. Unless you have the same thing I do."

"I did."

He blinked then his glance went to her legs as if looking for an obvious prosthesis.

"You won't find one," she said.

"Then we have nothing to talk about."

Adam rubbed the back of his neck. "Just hear her out."

"Don't need to. I already know what I want to do. I'm going home."

"You can't. Without treatment you will die."

"I'd like to see you or anyone else at this hospital try to stop me. I'd rather be dead than be without my leg. The other hospital said they'd have to take it." He gestured toward Sebastian, who was standing by the door. The stubborn set of Mr. Moreira's chin was probably there to disguise his fear. "Even you said there was no guarantee I could keep it."

Natália stepped into the patient's line of sight to force him to deal with her. "Did they tell you about the possibility of limb-salvaging surgery?"

"Yes," said Adam. "We've already been through this."

The irritation in his voice was plain—not at her but at his patient. She could understand where he was coming from. On the surface it seemed ridiculous to allow cancer to take your life when it could be cured. But until Adam had walked a mile in the shoes of someone who'd been there, he could just keep his damned annoyance to himself.

She shot him a glare. "Maybe he should

hear it from someone who's had the surgery."

Up went Adam's brows. Oh, he needn't have bothered claiming he had no idea what she was about to say. She had no illusions as to why he had brought her up here from the NICU. She focused on the patient instead. "I've had the surgery."

"I don't believe you. You don't walk with a limp or anything."

"It's true. The surgery wasn't on my leg, though." Natália tried to make her words as sincere as possible. "They found osteosarcoma in my left arm when I was a teenager. I'd had pain for a while, and by the time they discovered the cause, the tumor was quite large."

The patient's eyes went to her hand and then traveled up to where her forearm was hidden by the sleeve of her sweater.

She glanced at Sebastian and Adam. "Will you guys give me a few minutes alone with him? I want to—"

"If you think I'm going to change my mind because of a pretty lady with a fancy degree, you're wrong. If I can't ride a horse and do my job, I won't have the surgery. Even if it puts me in a hole in the ground."

"But what if you could still do things like ride and work cattle?"

"Natália!" Sebastian's curt use of her name held a wealth of warning. He didn't want her to make promises that couldn't be kept when his patient finally got to the operating table. Which would only come after several grueling rounds of chemotherapy to shrink the tumor.

Her brother could have saved himself the trouble. She wouldn't give his patient anything more than the truth—and tell him her own story. But didn't this man deserve to hear about a successful outcome? Yes, she'd had to give up her dreams of being a neurosurgeon due to her dexterity issues, but she was still a doctor. She'd had to make some changes, but she was no longer sad about it. She loved her job. And if she couldn't have children, surely it was the next best thing: to help thousands of little ones get off to the best possible start.

Mr. Moreira needed to know that if things went well, he wouldn't be resigned to sitting on the sofa for the rest of his life. She knew how hard these cowboys worked and how much of their identity was wrapped up in their jobs. That she could understand. She was built the exact same way.

She took a deep breath and then touched his hand. The man was a complete stranger, and yet she understood what was going on with him more than she understood Adam, who she'd known almost her entire life. "Tell them you'll talk to me."

The sun-weathered stretch of the man's throat moved as he swallowed. "Okay. I'll listen, but I won't make any promises."

"I'm not asking for any." She sent a pointed glance to Sebastian and Adam, since neither of them had budged from their spots. "Gentlemen?"

Adam was the first to push through the door, holding it for Sebastian, who gave her one last scowl. "We are going to have a discussion later." Then they were gone, leaving her to either perform that miracle they were looking for…or walk away in defeat.

Adam waited until the door was closed. "Do you think she can do it?"

"You know my sister. She is nothing if not mule-headed."

He leaned a shoulder against the wall. "We're looking at a year's worth of difficult treatment. And that's if everything goes according to plan."

"I know. Anything can happen in a year. Or even in a few weeks. As you well know." Sebastian eyed him. "Speaking of a few weeks, is there something you'd like to tell me?"

"Excuse me…?"

"You've been an ass for the last week or so. You even skipped out on our beer night yesterday. I was hoping you had a ton of girls squabbling over you and keeping you up until all hours like you used to. Meaning you're finally over what happened with Priscilla?"

Adam's jaw tightened into a hard knot. What he didn't need right now was a reminder of those days of playing the field, thinking he was invincible…that nothing bad could touch him. It had. His marriage had borne some of the brunt of that. He'd wanted lots of children almost immediately, maybe to assuage his guilt.

Hell, and then he'd had to go and kiss Natália. Which was exactly why he'd canceled his weekly trip to the bar. If he'd known his friend was going to make such a big deal about it, though, he would have gone and drowned the hell out of his sorrows.

"There is no girl—or girls—and Priscilla is over and done with. It's been a busy week at the hospital, that's all."

"Really? I asked Nata if she'd noticed anything, and she gave me some weird-ass answer."

"Weird? In what way?" Oh, hell, had she said something about him walking in on her in the exam room? Or worse?

Sebastian turned and looked him in the eye. "You would tell me if there was someone, wouldn't you? I worry about you. About Natália too, for that matter."

"I don't think she would appreciate you grilling her about her love life the way you're hounding me."

"I'm not 'hounding' anyone. I'm just being a good brother. And a friend." He smacked the back of Adam's head, like he used to do when they were younger. Except today he didn't find it funny.

Kissing Natália had been a one-off occurrence. He didn't want Sebastian or anyone else finding out about it. His friend hadn't exactly hinted that he should stay away from his sister, but he could read between the lines.

Or maybe those lines were from *his* book and not Sebastian's. It didn't matter. It was never happening again. Both he and Natália had agreed on that. Anything else would be idiocy. And a sure-fire way to ruin his friendship with both Natália and Sebastian. It wasn't worth it.

"I think what happens with your sister is her business." And that had *not* come out right.

"I just don't want her getting hurt. If I found out that someone did just that, I might have to…"

The implied threat raised his hackles. "You might have to what, exactly."

"My fist might have to find that person's face."

The words were even enough, but he'd turned up the volume a bit.

"Natália is all grown up. You know that, right?"

"I do. But I'm still her big brother." Sebastian shook his head as if to clear it, then one side of his mouth lifted. "Damn, sorry about that. I'm preaching to the choir, since you're practically her brother too."

His friend was right on one count but, oh, so wrong on the other. His behavior over the last week had not been that of a brother. Not even close. And Natália *had* had that girlhood crush on him. Had he taken advantage of that to get what he wanted?

Hell, he'd wanted a whole lot more than a simple kiss. Not that there had been anything simple about it. He gave the best response he could think of at the moment.

"I would never knowingly allow Natália to be hurt."

Sebastian nodded, dropping his hand from Adam's shoulder. "I know that. I just would hate for anything to—"

The door opened and the woman herself appeared. In the process of rolling down her left sleeve, her eyes shot fire. "You two yahoos know that these rooms are not completely soundproof, don't you?"

Adam shifted and forced a laugh. "Eavesdroppers never hear anything good about themselves, haven't you heard? I certainly didn't listen to what *you* were saying in there."

"Maybe because my voice wasn't raised. What were you two fighting about?"

"We weren't fighting." This time it was

Sebastian who spoke, a conciliatory tone to his voice that he'd used on his sister more than once. Wrong move. Natália had never taken kindly to someone trying to pat her on the head.

"Cut the act. We have more important things to talk about." She motioned toward the door behind her. "I think *your patient* has something he wants to tell you."

She was right. What was going on with their patient was life or death. Unlike the petty discussion he and Sebastian had been involved in. "You're right, Nata."

Her eyes softened for just an instant, before she glanced back at her brother and jerked her chin a little higher. "That goes for you, too."

"Seems to me that you always win these arguments."

"Not always."

Once they were next to the patient's bed, she put her hand on the man's arm. "Tell them what you told me."

Mr. Moreira glanced up at each of them. "She tells me I might not lose my leg." His mouth twisted. "At least not all of it. I know you already explained it but, well, she helped me understand."

Thank God the man had said "might." Sebastian had been worried about Natália painting pictures of flowers and clear skies. It sounded like she'd chosen her words carefully.

"If things go the way we hope they will, there's a possibility that we can insert a prosthetic device inside your leg rather than go with straight amputation."

"You'll take just the bone and replace it with a metal rod. Is that it?"

Sebastian stepped a little closer to his sister. "That's a simplistic explanation but, yes, it's what we see as a best-case scenario."

"And the worst-case scenario?"

"I think you already know what that is."

The man nodded. "Yes. I do. Talk to me a little more about this leg-saving surgery. What happens exactly?"

Adam went through the process as quickly as possible, while giving a global summary of the pros and cons.

"And it would be strong? This metal piece?"

"Stronger than your actual bone. That's not to say that it can't tear away during a bad accident."

"Or a fall off a horse?" Mr. Moreira's

hand went to the spot where the cancer had eaten away the bone in his leg.

"Yes." Adam wasn't willing to sugarcoat it.

"Hell, my last spill was bad enough that my leg could have snapped without there being any cancer involved."

"I heard it was pretty serious." Adam had seen quite a few broken bones caused by riding accidents over the years. But there were inherent risks in everything. In short, living itself was a dangerous affair.

"This...probos...what was it called again?"

"Prosthesis."

He waved away the word like it wasn't important, his attention going to Natália. "I'll be able to use my leg the same way I always have?"

"Almost," she answered. "Sometimes there are limitations. For example, I can't completely straighten my arm. Only about this much." Extending her joint as far as she could, she demonstrated her range of motion. She lacked about ten degrees from getting the limb completely straight. "But with your upper leg, it would be different. From what I understand, the tumor doesn't involve the knee or hip joints, so your prosthesis would just make up for the bone lost in surgery."

She glanced at Adam as if looking for confirmation of what she'd said.

Sebastian spoke up before he could. "Your tumor is in the central portion of your femur. I'm hoping we won't have to touch the knee at all."

"This is your sister?" Mr. Moreira jabbed his thumb at Natália.

"Yes."

"And you would do this surgery on her, if she had my type of cancer?"

Sebastian wouldn't be the one doing the surgery at all. Adam would. And the thought of having Natália go under his surgeon's scalpel made a roll of nausea go through him.

Thankfully he didn't have to answer the question. His friend did it for him. "Yes, I would recommend the same procedure. Don't forget I was there as she went through the entire process. It was hard, but she's strong. Probably as strong as you *gaúchos* are."

The patient laughed for the first time. "We are a pretty tough breed."

Natália gave his arm one last squeeze and

then let him go. "You would have to be careful, and it'll be a while before they know your exact limitations, but I haven't heard either of these doctors mention a reason for not riding a horse. I lift weights regularly to keep my bones strong enough to support my prosthesis. Your job is naturally weight-bearing, so you might not even have to do that."

"I don't know what weight-bearing means, but if you mean it'll take hard work...well, hell, that's about the only thing I know how to do."

"So you'll agree to treatment?" Sebastian took his tablet from the pocket of his coat and scrolled through a couple of screens.

"Yes. On one condition."

The oncologist frowned, his finger poised over his device. "What's that?"

"Your sister seems to be a straight shooter—kind of like my wife was. So I want to be able to talk to her. During my appointments. And before you start carving up my leg."

"I don't think that's going to be—"

"She's been through this. She'll know what's normal and what's not. She'll tell me if I need to start worrying, if I've read her right."

"It's okay, Sebastian." She stopped whatever her brother had been about to say with an uplifted hand. "I'll be here. And, yes, both of these men can tell you I'm pretty blunt."

Pretty blunt? The woman had as much tact as an elevator car with its cables cut.

Adam lifted a brow. "You don't want to get on her bad side, that's for sure." The last thing he wanted was to have Natália looking over his shoulder at every turn. But that wouldn't happen for a while. She'd be looking over her brother's for the first several months until chemo was completed. A lot could happen between then and surgery, but to wish her away would be to hope for a bad outcome for his patient, and Adam wouldn't do that. He would just have to power through it. Somehow.

"I have to agree with Dr. Cordeiro on this one. My sister is something else." Sebastian clapped Adam on the back. This time the gesture didn't carry any undertones other than friendship.

"Tell me where to sign then. The sooner this is over with the sooner I can get back to my *tereré*. This hospital doesn't even serve it."

Adam chuckled. "You probably wouldn't want it if they *did* serve it. It wouldn't be like what you can get back home."

Made by infusing a mixture of herbs called *erva mate*, *tereré* was popular among the cowboys and in several parts of Brazil and Paraguay. The passing of the *tereré* cup around a campfire had come to symbolize friendship and camaraderie. Since dozens of people might drink from the same flared metal straw, Adam could see why the hospital would frown on serving the chilled beverage.

"We might be able to find you something, though." Adam's family had originated from southern Brazil, and while his parents had been perfectionists who'd criticized their son for most of his choices, they'd passed on a love of their culture—like *mate* and *tereré*. So, he knew where to find the packaged herbs here in São Paulo. And the ornately carved gourds and straws were pretty ubiquitous.

He glanced up to find Natália's brown eyes on him, a soft smile playing on those luscious lips. His body sent a signal to his brain, which sent back a response, beginning a dangerous process.

Sebastian cleared his throat, looking from Adam to Natália. "I'm not sure Santa Coração will let you bring that in."

Damn. His friend hadn't missed that glance. Adam was going to have to watch himself like a hawk.

And not a sensory-deprived hawk either, because that would just make things worse.

"What the hospital doesn't know won't hurt them."

"No, but it might hurt you." Sebastian handed a form to Mr. Moreira along with a pen.

Was he imagining things? Or was there a hint of a threat behind those words? If so, Adam wasn't going to take the bait. He was just going to let it sit there and rot.

"A risk I'm willing to take." In fact, as big a mistake as kissing Natália might have been, he wouldn't go back and undo it, even if he could. He might not be willing or able to repeat it, but he had found himself reliving it in his head. Over and over. And each time her lips found his, the memory got sweeter.

Sebastian gave an irritable shrug and took

the clipboard back from his patient, glancing at it to make sure he had everything he needed. "I'll take these and get the process started. Don't stay long, you two. Our patient needs his rest."

Our patient.

His, Sebastian's and now Natália's. All he could see was them going round and round and round in circles. How this was going to work, he had no idea. But he and Natália had better figure out how to collaborate so that Mr. Moreira didn't have to suffer for their stupidity. That meant no more kissing her...or picturing the way she'd looked in that exam room.

But if she kept throwing him glances like the one she'd given him a few minutes earlier, that was going to be damned near impossible. So he'd have to give her a reason to be mad and stay mad.

All he had to do was come up with something they would both believe.

CHAPTER FIVE

"WHAT DO YOU mean I have to promise not to say anything negative to our patient?" Natália could not believe he had just stood there and told her to basically lie to the man. She was so not having it!

"As you know, a patient's attitude can affect the outcome so I would prefer that you—"

"Paint a yellow brick road and not crap in the middle of it. Is that it?"

Adam shut the door to the exam room and then crossed his arms over his chest. "Nice image, thanks for shouting it down the hallway."

"It's the one that came to mind. Sorry if it offends your delicate sensibilities. Some of us have learned to take negative comments and deal with them."

"Such as?"

"Never mind."

"Maybe you shouldn't be involved with this case after all. Especially since Sebastian is breathing threats about going after anyone who hurts you."

Her breath caught with an audible pop that he had to have heard. "Why? Did you say something to him?"

"No, I think it was a general statement. You said you heard it."

"I heard Sebastian say something about punching someone. He wasn't threatening *you*, was he?"

Adam's hands went to his hips, thumbs hooking over the waistband of his pants. "No. But I don't want to give him any ideas."

"Such as? It's not like we're involved or anything." And the man had made it clear that they never would be either.

"No, but if you insist on staying on this case, we'll have to be around each other—a lot more than normal—and…well, Sebastian might draw the wrong conclusion if he sees us conferring in an exam room."

Conferring? Was he talking about when he'd burst in on her unannounced? That was hardly a planned meeting.

"That's ridiculous."

How humiliating this must be for Adam, having to make sure it didn't look like he was playing around with the little sister. Nothing could be further from the truth. The only thing that had passed between them was a momentary flare of lust. He would have reacted the same way to any other woman who had flashed her underwear at him.

You didn't flash them, you dope. It was an accidental exposure, like when you forget to go behind the screen when performing an X-ray.

Something about that thought made her laugh.

"I'm glad you find this whole thing so amusing."

The laugh rolled back inside her. "I don't. Is that what this is about, though? You want me to drop off the case to make this easier for you?" She paused to regroup her thoughts. It would make it easier. For both of them. That didn't make it the right thing to do, though. "I'm sorry, Adam. That's not going to happen. This isn't about me. Or you. Or even Sebastian and his psychotic need to protect someone who *does not* need protecting. It's about a patient whose life could depend on us figuring out how to play nicely together."

A muscle pulsed in his cheek a time or two before going still. "You're right. I reminded Sebastian of that very thing."

"Thank you."

"Anyway, my thought wasn't to have you lie to our patient, but just to emphasize the positive rather than dwell on the negative."

"I walked through this, Adam. That in and of itself has equipped me to see things that someone else might not be able to. I lived through the fear, the surgeries, through the horror of someone hinting that it might be easier if I were just…gone."

The words came faster and faster, and she had to bite her lip to staunch anything else that might slip out. Why the hell had she said that last thing? She'd never told anyone what she'd overheard her father say in a fit of anger. *God!*

"Que…?" He gripped her arm. "Who said that to you, Nata?"

"It doesn't matter."

"Was it Sebastian?"

"No, of course not. Why would you even think that?"

He cocked his head, grip tightening

slightly. "It would explain why he is so over-protective. Maybe he's working through some kind of guilt complex."

The way he said that made the hair at her nape stand at attention. "It wasn't Sebastian. And it was a long time ago. I don't even know why I mentioned it, except to say that I think I can help on this case. Please let me."

Adam released his grip, hand sliding down her arm until the tips of his fingers touched hers. "I hate that we're having to ask at all. Sebastian mentioned it might dredge up painful memories. Are you sure you're up to that?"

There was no way to answer that, because she didn't know.

His fingers slid higher, tickling her palm as they wrapped around her hand and squeezed. "You're stronger than anyone I know, Nata, and I can't imagine what this world would be like if you weren't in it. Whoever said that to you should be hung, drawn and quartered."

"He didn't mean it. Not really. It was a really tough time in my famil—"

"Hell, you can't be serious. If it wasn't Sebastian… Your *father* said that to you?"

"No. Not to me—he would never do that.

He said it to my mom. I just happened to be on the other side of the door. You said it yourself: 'Eavesdroppers never hear anything good about themselves.' I think he felt helpless, and it just exploded one day. It's not the first time someone has talked about me when I was in the next room."

"Me and Sebastian."

She answered with a nod. His thumb trailed over the back of her hand. "I'm sorry, sweetheart. Sebastian and I were both being asses for having that discussion there."

"You were asses for having it at all. My personal life is none of your business. It's none of Sebastian's business."

That crooked smile that used to make her tremble shifted into place. "It's kind of hard to stay completely out of it when I was in the room, participating in it." His grip tightened. "Or don't you remember?"

She remembered everything. The pressure of his mouth on hers, the rough sound of their breathing as the kiss deepened. The way parts of her softened…moistened…hoping for things to end a very different way.

Damn, she would have let him make love to her that night, she was so far gone. And yet Adam hadn't been anywhere near that point. He'd been able to move away with an ease that drove the wind from her lungs and sent heat pouring into her face.

Still, Sebastian had no right to question her choices as long as she wasn't hurting anyone.

Or was she? Wasn't she hurting herself by letting her emotions carry her down dark roads?

Yes. But one small mistake did not a ruined life make.

They'd stopped before it was too late. And they were both fine. Their friendship was still intact, even. It might be straining a bit at the seams, but it had at least lived to tell the tale. And if they'd gone further than they had?

She didn't know.

What she did know was that she wanted to help Adam and Sebastian with this case. "When exactly will he start treatment?"

"At this point, the sooner the better, since that fracture is going to have to be addressed."

"My arm never broke. It just hurt like the devil, which is why my parents took me in to have it checked out." She rubbed the area that lay just beneath her sleeve. "Thank God they did."

His fingers traveled up to where her hand was, his light touch sizzling across her senses in a way that was not good. Hadn't she just lectured herself about not letting him get to her?

"I've only seen your scar a couple of times," he murmured. "Did you show it to the patient?"

Natália swallowed as the air in the room got even thicker. "Yes. He needed to see it."

"And if I needed to see it, what would you do?"

If she thought she'd been imagining the change in him, his low words would have made a believer out of her. Was this because of what she'd told him about her father? Maybe. Because there was suddenly an intimacy between them that was almost palpable.

She breathed the words. "I would show it to you."

"Show me, then. Please, Natália."

Lord, she was suddenly standing on shaky ground, trying to find her footing. It wasn't as if he'd asked her to undress, and yet he might as well have. She showed her scar to almost no one outside her doctors. Sebastian had seen it, and her parents, of course. But outside her family? Not so much. She hadn't been a fan of flashing it around. Her mom had said she should be proud of it—it was the scar from a battle she'd won. Natália, however, had always seen it as a sign that her body had let her down. A stupid belief.

But she wanted to show Adam again. And she had no idea why.

Her sweater had three-quarter-length sleeves. She wasn't going to take it off, that was for sure. Been there, done that…in the opposite order.

As she stood there, trying to figure out how to go about it, Adam captured her wrist and held her arm out from her body. "May I?"

She had to settle for nodding, because the air now seemed stuck in her lungs and no amount of pushing would get it to budge.

Gently, he reached for the sleeve to her sweater and rolled it over and over, until it was up past her elbow, revealing the stark white scar along the inner side of her arm. She was among those unfortunate souls whose skin lost pigmentation wherever it was injured. She'd always hated that it hadn't blended in better as it healed, but instead it sent up a neon sign announcing its presence.

Which was part of the reason she kept it covered up.

Mr. Moreira had been surprised by how small it was. Just under six inches, it still looked huge to her. She'd warned him that his scar might be larger, due to the fact that his tumor was on his leg. "That don't matter. I don't spend my days laying around a beach trying to get one of them suntans. And if it helps me keep my leg, I don't care if it's twenty inches long and ugly as sin." His words had made her smile.

Adam's thumb slid up to the spot and then touched her, a bare whisper, but it ignited her senses even further. "It's dainty. Feminine. Like you."

Dainty and feminine? Her scar?

Okay, when he touched her like that, he could call it anything he liked. Her eyelids fluttered closed, while Adam continued to explore, moving up past her elbow joint to where the scar ended. Then he headed back down, gliding along the line with aching slowness. Her breathing hitched for a second before resuming.

"This scar means you are still here. Still making a difference in people's lives. In my life."

God, how could those simple words light up her insides like a torch? But they did.

And his touch...

She swallowed.

"Nata."

It was coming. She knew it was. Because it was exactly the same way he'd said her name on the night he'd kissed her.

Her eyes reopened to find him leaning over the site. And then his lips found it, and she gasped as the heat of his mouth moved over her cool skin.

Her free hand went to the back of his head, her fingers curling in his hair, not wanting him to move away from this spot. Yet she knew he would. Knew he wasn't going to make love to her in an unlocked exam room. But, oh, how she wanted him to.

If he stopped this time, she was going to be crushed. But what choice was there?

She didn't know. Couldn't think. And Adam seemed in no hurry to walk away from her.

And she was in no hurry to ask him to stop.

Then his arm was around her back and

he was yanking her to him. Down came his mouth, covering hers with an urgency that matched what had been building inside her for the last couple of minutes.

Winding her arms around his neck, she leaned fully into him, coming up against the vivid effect she was having on him.

The feeling was mutual.

His hands glided down to her hips, securing her in place while his lips left hers and trailed along her cheek until he reached the side of her neck. When his teeth scraped the skin, it sent a shudder of need arcing through her.

Locked door or not, she wanted him. Right now.

Maybe he sensed what she was thinking, or maybe he was thinking the same thing himself, because he wrapped an arm beneath her butt and hauled her up against himself. Then walking toward another small door just off to the side, he opened it. Moving inside the tiny space, he did the unthinkable: he locked the door.

The bathroom. She hadn't thought of that, but it would work. Right now, she didn't care where they went. She spied the "pull for help" cord and a quick smile went through her. She'd better try to remember that was there. The last thing she wanted was for twenty people to come tearing down the hall to see what was wrong.

"Turn around."

She blinked up at him, then his hands were back on her hips, urging her to turn away from him.

They were going to do this. They were really going to do this.

When his fingers moved to the hem of her skirt and slid up the backs of her bare thighs, she couldn't prevent herself from leaning her torso slightly forward to give him more access. He took the invitation and ran with it, reaching higher until he found the elastic waist of her underwear and pulled them down with a quick decisive movement that made her moan.

"Shh." His lips went to her ear. "I'm going to need you to be very, very quiet, Nata."

Quiet? Was he kidding? She wanted to cry and scratch and beg, and make him take her quick and hard.

Cool air whispered across her butt and she heard the soft snick of a zipper being lowered. She licked her lips, her eyelids slamming shut in anticipation. "Don't worry about a condom. I can't get pregnant."

There was silence for several long seconds. Just as she began to worry, his teeth nipped her earlobe hard. "Shh...remember?"

His hands covered her breasts, and even with her thin sweater and bra separating them, her nipples tightened in response, sending fire straight down to her center. Lord, at this rate, she might explode before he even got to the main event.

"You're gorgeous, Nata. If we had time, I would kiss every last inch of you. As it is..."

His whispered words trailed away as he used his upper body to coax hers forward until she was bent at the waist. Reaching around to the front of her, one hand slipped between her legs and found that sensitive bit of flesh which was already pulsing with mad heat. She started to moan again and then remembered his warning and bit her lip—hard—to prevent any sound from escaping.

A knee touched the back of one of hers and nudged it sideways, urging her to spread her legs. She did. Quickly. Eagerly.

And then his flesh slid down and forward until he found just the right spot.

Do it. Please.

His hips surged forward. Hard. Until he was fully inside her. He stayed there, holding himself in that position with a delicious pressure that sent a jolt of something through her. She waited for him to move. To do anything. But he didn't.

She shifted slightly, wondering if something was wrong. He shifted with her.

"Um-uh. Too easy."

"What?"

"I'm not going to move, and you're going to come."

The words were simple enough, but they didn't register for a second or two, but when they did...

No! She wanted him to repeat that first hard thrust. To take everything that had been building up inside her and make it go off in a delicious explosion.

She tried edging forward, but he matched every move with one of his own, so that there was no back-and-forth friction. None. Just that steady pressure inside, his arm now wrapped around her waist.

She was dying. Wanted him to touch her. Anywhere. To release the floodgates and let her go.

"Adam—"

"Shh. Give it a minute."

A minute? She wanted satisfaction now!

The pressure morphed, and her senses, on high alert for any type of movement, went crazy. It didn't come. But her mind imagined it a thousand different ways. Pumping furiously into her. Sliding with aching slowness until she could stand it no longer.

The pressure.

Her insides quivered. Tensed.

Ah. Wait! That was it. She squeezed her inner muscles again, feeling his whole length as she did.

He bit her earlobe, as if rewarding her for what she'd discovered. She tightened around him, the luscious sensation making her quicken the pace, while that nub at the juncture of her thighs reacted with a short spasm.

Yes!

She bent slightly more to change the angle and clenched those muscles again and again, his breathing growing ragged as she experimented with different ways of gripping him. Tighter. Longer. Harder.

"*Deus*… Nata…"

Close. She was getting so close. If he touched her, she would go off in an instant.

But she didn't need him to. That pressure against her cervix had made her super-sensitized. She clutched and squeezed, the earth beginning to spin at light speed. Whirling, tilting, pulsing, until...

Her body convulsed, her nervous system hijacking her thoughts and stealing away all voluntary movement. And then Adam was thrusting madly, muttering words that made no sense at all as she hurtled through the stratosphere, heading for someplace she didn't recognize.

He pumped and pumped, until his frenetic pace of a few seconds ago began to gradually slow, the tilting world righting itself as he drew to a halt. His arm tightened around her waist, holding her in place, maybe to keep her from falling. Or maybe to keep himself from keeling over too.

A huge wave of lethargy washed over her, carrying her slowly back to terra firma. The place where she'd started. And she'd never felt so...complete.

He'd done it. Adam had made love to her.

Never in a million years would she have imagined it could be like this. And...

And, oh, Lord. She was in trouble.

She'd been worried about losing his

friendship over a kiss? What was going to happen now? She squeezed her eyes shut, trying to figure some logical way out of this that would put them back to where they should be.

It was just physical. Simply a much-needed release of tension after an incredibly difficult week. Then there'd been that patient. And the admission about her father. Strong emotions were bound to bring out some male/female urges. It was natural.

Normal.

Really? *Really?*

Her brain went into overdrive, sucking down energy at an enormous rate as she tried to find an escape.

But there was nothing normal about what had just happened between them. Suddenly, she was very, very afraid. Was this why he'd wanted her to keep quiet? So he could picture himself here with someone else? Someone who wasn't like a kid sister?

That thought made her squelch inside.

"Adam?"

She wasn't sure if she was asking him if he was okay, or if she was looking for reassurance, but she needed to hear his voice.

"Give me a sec, okay?"

His voice was still rough, but this was not the same sexy, gravelly tone he'd used seconds earlier. He was trying to figure out how to get away from her.

Suddenly, it was Natália who was struggling to get away, to force him to pull out. He moved back in a hurry, separating them, and she reached down and grabbed her panties with jerky movements. Anything to get out of this room. Out of view.

Within seconds, she was dressed, her skirt pulled back into place as she rushed through the door. The last thing she heard as she fled was Adam's voice calling to her, telling her to wait.

But she couldn't wait. Wasn't sure she'd be able to face him ever again. So she wouldn't try. At least not today. And maybe not tomorrow.

She would give herself as long as it took to get this whole damn encounter out of her mind. And, more importantly, out of her heart.

CHAPTER SIX

WHY HAD SHE offered to have the baby shower at her house?

Because Maggie is your best friend, that's why.

Plus she'd been so busy with the last-minute preparations that she'd barely been able to think about that disastrous encounter with Adam.

Right. Keep on telling yourself that, Natália.

Truth be told, she'd barely been able to think about anything else. But at least the shower allowed her to put off the really hard questions, like *why*…and *what now*.

Pushing aside some streamers that had drifted in her path, she made her way over to Maggie, who was seated in a chair. The mom-to-be's face glowed with health and happiness, her hand laid across her belly.

She was pretty sure her friend had no idea that she was rubbing small circles over the bump as if her baby were right there instead of still tucked inside her body.

She dropped beside her friend and forced a bright smile. "Having fun?"

"Yes, thank you so much! We still have quite a few things left from Marcos Junior's birth a few years ago, but it's fun to celebrate each child." Her hand stopped rubbing. "We weren't sure we were going to be able to have another baby."

A pang went through her heart. "And now look at you."

She'd told Adam they didn't need a condom because, unlike her friend who'd had a little difficulty getting pregnant a second time, Natália had no illusions about her chances of having a baby. They were nonexistent, her eggs killed by her chemo treatments. Her smile wavered.

"Hey, are you okay?" Maggie looked into her face.

"I'm fine."

"I don't think so." Her friend wrapped an arm around her. "I'm sorry. I know this can't be easy. It's why I was reluctant to let you throw me the shower."

What wasn't? Knowing most of the women in this room had children? She shook off the pang of self-pity. This wasn't like her. She'd made peace with that part of her life a long time ago. So why was she suddenly going all melancholy?

"I'm okay, Mags. Really. I'm happier for you than you could ever know. If anyone deserves a healthy happy pregnancy, it's you."

"You deserve it too, honey. And I'm sorry…" She took a deep breath. "Why do you work in the preemie unit? Doesn't it hurt?"

Her friend knew about her situation. The scar on her arm seemed to ache all of a sudden.

"Sometimes." She shrugged. "But I love babies. If I can't have them then this gives me a way to love them. I can't imagine a more fulfilling job."

"But—"

"No buts." Natália turned and gave her friend a kiss on the cheek. "No feeling sad or sorry or anything else. I have a wonderful, fulfilling life, with the best friends a girl could have. I can't imagine anything better."

Not even an accidental pregnancy? Caused by a single slip-up?

And maybe wrangle a certain orthopedic surgeon into a proposal?

No. Not how she wanted things to happen. She and Adam were not a match made in heaven. He wanted kids. Lots of kids. Sebastian had told her that was what had broken up his marriage to Priscilla: she didn't want kids and he did.

Maggie stretched her back. "Well, you'll be godmother to this little one too, right?"

Godparenting was serious business in Brazil, and although Maggie wasn't native to the country, she had embraced her life here. And she and Marcos were unbelievably happy and in love.

Which was what Nata wanted when she finally found someone.

If. *If* she found someone.

"I would be upset if you didn't ask." She gave her friend's hand a squeeze. "Did you guys finally decide on a name?"

"I think so. Carolina is the top pick at the moment."

"I love it!"

Just then a couple of squeals came from somewhere on the other side of the room, followed by some laughter. Since she was sitting next to Maggie she couldn't exactly figure out what was going on, but as long as her guests were having a good time…

Ding-ding-ding. Ding-ding-ding.

Someone was ringing what sounded like the kind of bell found on the counter of a hotel lobby. What in the world…?

"Hey, everyone, can I get your attention?"

She still couldn't see what was happening, but since alcohol had been banned from this gathering because Maggie wasn't allowed to drink, it couldn't be anything bad. Maybe they were ready to open the gifts.

The noise died down, people turning toward the speaker. A basket appeared in front of her. "Take one and write your name on it, please."

The woven bowl had a bunch of red cut-outs in it. Only after she'd taken one out did she realize it was a pair of lips. "What's this?"

Maggie took a pair too. "This looks like fun. What did you do, Nata?"

"I didn't do anything, and this doesn't look like one of the games I planned."

The woman with the basket, a nurse from the neonatal department, laughed. "A few of us got together and planned a very special event." She winked at Maggie and then handed her a permanent marker. "Write your names on them, please."

When she balked, Maggie grabbed the pen and wrote her name on one of the cutouts and then took Natália's and did the same, before dropping the pen back into the basket. The nurse flounced away, headed for her next victims.

"I don't like this."

Maggie patted her hand. "It's fine."

Something about the way she said that made Natália glance suspiciously at her friend. "Wait. Is this *your* doing?"

"Maybe." Maggie laughed. "I may be pregnant, but I'm not dead."

"What is that supposed to mean?"

"It means that we have some very hunky men working at our hospital. Several of them are unattached."

The bell began dinging again. "Okay, everyone have a seat, please."

People wandered to scattered chairs and the couch, the sea of heads slowly receded, revealing...

"Oh, my God."

Across the far wall were a bunch of men. Only they weren't alive. They were cut out of some kind of poster board or something. She recognized most of the faces. Doctors from various wards had been propped up, the headshots from a hospital pamphlet pasted onto bodies with bare muscular chests. They all wore the same pair of red board shorts. And nothing else.

Natália gulped. There in the middle of the grouping was Adam's face. She glanced at the pair of lips in her hand.

Oh, this wasn't good. Not good at all. But since Maggie had evidently had a hand in it, it wasn't like she could override her colleagues and demand they stop at once.

"So," said Marissa Cleo, the ringleader and also a doctor. "You've all played pin the tail on the *burro* at some point as a kid, right?"

The question was met with a bunch of nods and a few whistles.

"Well, we have a very adult version of that game, just for us girls, called Pin the Lips on the Surgeon."

More laughter ensued. Marissa talked over them. "Quiet down, ladies. Let me give you the rules and then we can get down to business."

The "rules" were as bad as she'd feared. There were blindfolds involved. And the double-sided tape she hadn't noticed on her set of lips was to be used to secure them to one of the doctors on display. Panic flooded her system. She squashed it down.

Okay, no need to have a stroke. She searched the row of men and found the oldest of the bunch, a neurosurgeon who, although in his late fifties, was still very much a silver fox. But at least he was on the far left hand side of the pack, and since Adam's cutout was on the right, there was no danger that she would somehow put her lips on his…anything.

"And now for the final rule. After each person has kissed their doc…" More laughter. "We are going to mix up the contestants. No fair, choosing your favorite ahead of time."

Damn!

Maggie suddenly stood to her feet and headed across the room. "Just a minute. I need to make a slight adjustment." She went up to the cardboard cutout of her husband and picked it up, laying it over her shoulder, shooting a mock glare at Marissa. "I don't know how he got mixed up in this group of

single men, but he is most definitely taken.
And no one's lips are going to land on my
man, except for mine."

A chorus of *aww*s went up around the
room. If only she could march over and
snatch Adam's image and say the same
thing—except for the "her lips" thing. Because she did *not* want her lips to wind up
on him. If they were going to shuffle the
cutouts in between players then she would
just make sure she went high. As in aim for
the hair. A sisterly kiss on the head. Or even
on the wall behind them.

Oh, that's good. She could do that. Since
the heads were all pasted onto the same cutout, they were all the same height. She was
safe.

"The first contestant is the party girl herself. Come on up, Maggie." Marissa grinned.
"Although since you've taken your husband
off the docket, that means you might end up
cheating on him with one of our other handsome colleagues."

"Oh, no." She took her lips and placed
them on Marcos's smiling face. "I am off
the docket as well."

Everyone except for Natália found that
hilarious. She was no longer laughing or

even smiling as person after person played the game.

Adam had his first hit. Someone's lips landed on his left shoulder. She cringed. Another person's landed in the middle of his chest. On his eyebrow. Just like the old days when he'd shown up at events with a different woman on his arm.

Suddenly she didn't feel quite so special. Or that their time in that bathroom was any different than a multitude of other quick encounters.

She swallowed. Maybe it was a good thing that she hadn't seen him—even in passing—over the last two days. And right now she didn't care if she never saw him again.

"Natália, come on up."

She shook her head, trying to get out of it. Marissa nudged her with her shoulder. "Come on, it's just a game."

No, it wasn't. But unless she wanted to explain what it was that made it feel so deadly real, she would have to play along.

Trudging up to the front, she let herself be blindfolded and spun around three times, knowing that there was some mad shuffling going on up front with those cutouts.

Aim high. Very high.

"Okay, Nata, walk straight ahead."

The lips in her hand, she shuffled her feet, edging to the left and hopefully away from the line-up of men. Hands went to her shoulders and righted her path, then stopped her at a certain point.

"All right, girlie, kiss your man."

Damn. Her sense of direction was all screwed up, but this could still work. She just needed to raise her hand as high over her head as she could and… She jabbed the lips onto the first thing she came in contact with and hoped for the best. The laughter was instantaneous and…too raucous to mean anything good. Reaching her hand forward to see if she could tell where they had landed, she felt something flip out of her pocket. Whatever it was hit the tile floor and made an all too ominous cracking sound.

Adam knocked on the door. He'd spent the last two days trying to figure out a way to do this that didn't involve apologizing. His head was a mass of conflicting emotions and snatches of memories. Of Nata…and him… and that damned bathroom.

He was eventually going to run into her at the hospital, and that was the last place he wanted to have this kind of discussion. So here he was. Standing outside her door. Getting no response.

He knocked again. Harder this time.

A second later, the door was flung open and sounds of wild laughter thumped him in the chest. A woman he vaguely recognized stood there, her eyes suddenly going wide. "Um…hello there."

He'd better come back later. "I didn't know Natália had company. Sorry I'll come back another—"

Against his better judgment his glance went past the woman and he frowned. The room was packed with people. Females. There were pink and blue balloons everywhere and… Men?

Not men, exactly. They looked like life-sized ad posters of some type. And he—oh, hell—he knew them. All of them. A woman at the front was just taking off a blindfold and reaching down to scoop something up off the floor, grimacing at whatever it was.

And the woman at the door waved wildly and then pointed at him. The laughter began dying away until the room was silent. The person with the blindfold turned toward him.

Nata.

He should just turn around and walk away, but something made him step into the foyer of her house.

Her eyes met his and the blood drained from her face, her head swiveling back toward the row of men, one of which was being held directly in front of her. His face was on it, but those bulky muscles were definitely not his. The woman dropped the cutout and inched away from it.

Suddenly there was a choreographed rush of movement as women began gathering their belongings and saying their goodbyes as they filed out of the door. Nervous laughter and smiles accompanied the mass exodus. Someone muttered an apology as they went past.

He could see why.

Through it all, Natália hadn't moved a muscle. She stood right where she was.

Then it was just him. And her. And...was that Maggie? Yes. Natália's friend had gotten up and was standing beside her. Before he could say anything, Maggie held up her hand to stop him. Which was funny, because he was pretty much speechless right now.

"Just so you know, this wasn't Natália's idea."

What wasn't? The party—which looked like one part baby shower, one part bachelorette party.

He glanced again at the cutouts, peering closer and noticing there were shapes—*were those lips?*—pasted on various parts of the men.

He focused on the one of him. There were five pairs of lips on it, each with someone's name scrawled across them. They were on his shoulders, his neck, his forehead, except for one pair. The pair labeled *Natália*. They were pasted squarely on his...

Oh, hell.

A shot of pure sensation hit the real-life part of his anatomy. He did his best to squash it, even as he heard a loud gasp. It wasn't Natália who made the sound but Maggie, and she was looking at the floor where a puddle had formed.

"Okay, guys. No more time for chit-chat." Her face was now as pale as her friend's. "I'm still four weeks away from my due date. And I think my water just broke."

* * *

Adam stood next to Natália in the hallway of the maternity wing as they waited on word about Maggie. He was feeling kind of shell-shocked after the crazy turn of events. First their frenetic session in the bathroom and then the baby shower.

He'd called himself every name in the book as he'd zipped himself back into his pants two days ago and had gone after her, but by the time he'd reached the bank of elevators, it was too late. Every door had already closed. He'd figured he should leave her alone for a day or two, so that's what he'd done.

He'd gone to her apartment with thoughts of rectifying his mistake, only to come across that surreal scene.

Why had she placed her set of lips on him? And why there? That did not sound like Natália at all. Unfortunately he'd never gotten the chance to ask her.

What the heaven, hell and every other place had he been thinking, dragging her into the restroom like that?

Something about Natália sharing the horrible thing her father had said about her and then willingly exposing her scar to him had ignited a slow burn in his gut that no amount of cold water could put out.

A ding from the elevator shifted his attention off his own problems. Until the doors opened, and exiting the car was the last person he wanted to see right now.

Sebastian. He'd managed to avoid his friend over the last couple of days as well. In fact, he'd hoped to have things straightened out with Natália before seeing him. That hadn't happened.

He headed straight toward them. "How is she?" he asked.

"We don't know anything yet." The worry in Natália's voice was obvious.

He wanted to put his arm around her, but didn't dare. Especially not with her brother standing in front of them.

"What are you doing here, Adam? I didn't think the rumor mill worked that fast."

She saved him from having to think of a plausible explanation by taking a step forward with her eyes narrowed. "That's kind of a rude question. Why does it matter? Maybe we were making out in one of the exam rooms when a nurse burst in on us and told us what happened."

Sebastian just stood there for a second, and then glanced his way. "Excuse me?"

Natália's face flamed with color, and she half stepped in front of him. "I'm joking. I was joking."

"Not funny, Nat. I think you owe Adam an apology."

The irony in those words struck him right between the eyes, since that's what he'd stopped by her apartment to do: apologize. Try to explain what had come over him, although there actually was no explanation for that. However, he had wanted to promise that he would never let anything like that happen again. And then he'd seen multiple lips plastered to a poster board cutout that sported a picture of his face.

He still hadn't received an explanation about that, and wasn't sure he wanted one. All he wanted was to keep his friendship with both Sebastian and Natália intact. Was that even possible at this point?

He and his ex-wife had been friends before they'd started dating. That friendship had been demolished over the course of their marriage. He did not want that to happen with him and Natália. The only way to fix things was to somehow dial back the clock to a time before he'd seen her in those silky underthings. That sudden shot of lust had been not only unacceptable, but despicable. He had to start thinking with something other than libido.

"I'm sorry, Adam. I don't know why I said that," she said.

He knew exactly why she'd said it. Because the best way to throw Sebastian off track was to hand him something so totally outrageous that no one in his right mind would believe it.

Adam said the only thing he could. "Don't worry about it."

Only he was worried. Very worried.

Sebastian's posture relaxed, even though his brows slid an inch or so higher on his forehead. "So how is Maggie?"

"They're going to take the baby. She's in surgery now."

He glanced toward the waiting room behind them. "And Marcos?"

Adam had met Marcos Pinheiro through Sebastian and Natália when they'd been teenagers. Maggie's husband had to be worried sick.

Natália nodded toward the doors at the end of the corridor. "He's with her. The baby is almost a month early, but when we got here, her blood pressure was so high they had to act fast."

"I'm sure it will be fine." He wasn't sure if he was trying to reassure Natália or himself. Because nothing else felt fine right now. He and Natália would eventually have to figure out how to move forward from this point. But he did not want that conversation to take place in front of her brother. Or in front of friends who were hoping their baby was going to be okay.

"I'm surprised you're not in there, Natália." Her brother glanced back at her.

"They already had a team in place, and since Maggie and I are good friends they thought that it was better if I stay out here."

There had been a little bit of a verbal skirmish about that with the obstetrician, but Nata had given in and agreed to let the on-duty staff handle it.

Just then the doors opened and a man in blue scrubs headed their way. Ah, Marcos.

Natália hurried forward. "How are they?"

"They're both fine. We have a little girl. Carolina Linda Pinheiro. She's amazing." His smile was genuine, even if it seemed a little shakier than he remembered.

"And Maggie? You said she's okay as well?"

"They're still waiting for her blood pressure to come down a little bit more, but they think the worst has passed."

Sebastian clapped his friend on the back. "Great news, *cara*. Your text message didn't give me much to go on. And then I tried to call Natália but it went straight to voicemail. Luckily she was already here."

"I dropped my phone, unfortunately." She pulled the device from her pocket and displayed the front, which had cracks radiating out from the center. "I can't even get it to power up."

"How does that even happen with protective cases nowadays?"

She shrugged. "I was in a hurry. It flipped out of my pocket when I was at the baby shower."

She hadn't said anything about breaking her phone. But he remembered seeing her pick something up off the floor. Right after she'd planted those lips on him. Someday, he would get that image out of his head. But right now his body was posing a question and waiting on a response. Well, that was an easy one to answer.

Never. He was never having sex with her ever again.

Maybe he would actually believe that at some point.

While Sebastian and Marcos continued to talk, Adam moved beside Natália, who had her lab coat back on, the sleeve pulled safely down her arm.

"Hey." He touched her hand. "You okay?"

Her head turned sharply in his direction. "Yep. It's been quite a week. But I'm still in one piece."

"Except for your phone." He took the device from her and studied the damage. "I know a guy—"

"Kind of like the guy you know who can fix cars?" She wrinkled her nose in a way that he recognized. Not quite rueful but not angry, either. "I think I'd better take care of this one myself. It's safer that way."

"Safer?"

"Never mind. Sorry for telling Sebastian we were making out. He has been impossible lately, and I didn't want to give him any ideas."

"About us?" He smiled. "Smart girl. I think it worked."

"Yeah, because no one in their right mind

would ever suspect you would go after someone like me."

He reeled backward in shock at the soft conviction in her voice. "What the hell would make you say something like that?"

"Something like what?" Sebastian and Marcos had turned back toward them.

Natália's teeth came down on her lip, and he could imagine her mind racing to think up something that didn't give them away.

"She's worried she won't be able to convince Mr. Moreira to continue with his treatments."

"What?" Sebastian frowned. "You did a great job with him from what I could tell."

"Thanks." She tugged at her sleeve. But the gesture that Adam had once found endearing gave him pause now. Was she really that self-conscious? Surely that wasn't why she'd said that about no one believing he would go after her.

Something else he would have to talk to her about. He looked at her, trying to see her through eyes that hadn't known her for most of his life.

He couldn't. She was beautiful. Truly gorgeous, but there was so much more to Natália than her looks. She was kind, feisty, and she would fight to the death for someone she cared about.

So why did she think he couldn't be attracted to her? Because of the way he used to chase party girls?

"Who is Mr. Moreira?" Marcos was staring at them, lost as to what they were talking about.

"He's a patient. Natália has been trying to steer him in the right direction. He has the same thing she once had."

"Osteosarcoma?"

Sebastian nodded. "It was kind of a godsend that he fell into our laps. He didn't want to do treatments at all…he'd convinced himself that his life was over."

"I can't think of anyone more equipped to help with that than Natália." Marcos smiled at her. "Maggie loves her like a sister. Speaking of which, the reason I came out here is that she wants to see you."

"Is she up to it?" Natália took a step away from him, and Adam didn't like the way that made him feel.

"She wants a second opinion on the baby, and she's pretty insistent when she sets her mind on something."

Kind of like Nata. Only she hadn't set her

mind on him. At least not for long. "I know someone else who is as well." Sebastian gave his sister a quick hug.

"I also believe in clinging to reality," she stated. "Not that that has anything to do with Maggie or little Carolina."

But it evidently had something to do with him. Maybe she was sending him the same message that he'd meant to give her. That he was sorry for what had happened, but knew better than to think that it should—or would—go any further than it already had.

In that case, he agreed completely.

They still needed to talk. But not this very second.

As Natália walked away from him for the second time in the last half-hour, he knew he was going to have to chase her down once again. Not now, but soon.

Because of all the things he might stand to lose, Nata's friendship was the one thing he couldn't afford to leave behind. Not without at least trying to make things right.

"She's perfect, Maggie." Natália's exam echoed what the attending neonatologist had said. Carolina was tiny, but the steroids they'd administered had sped up the development of her lungs, so she was breathing on her own with just a boost of oxygen to carry her through.

Her friend had no idea that she'd given Nata the escape route she'd been searching for out there in the waiting room. The last thing she wanted was to talk about their little rendezvous in the bathroom, or what Adam had seen at that baby shower.

That shower had been the wake-up call she'd needed. No matter how much she might wish things were different, they weren't. And they would never be.

So why had she ventured outside some of those known boundaries?

Because she'd wanted to. There was no other explanation.

And it was so ridiculous. She couldn't have kids, and she knew Adam wanted them. Desperately. He'd told her so once, when he'd been drunk out of his mind. That was a reality that she knew couldn't be flouted. No matter how hard she might try, the end result would be filled with heartache and disappointment.

Maggie's hand touched hers. "Are you sure she's okay?"

"I wouldn't lie to you." Natália might lie

to herself, but she would never tell Maggie something that wasn't true. Not about something so important. "Marcos Junior has a perfect baby sister."

"I'm so glad." Maggie's head fell back against the pillows. "When my water broke at the shower, I was sure something was wrong. And then they rushed out of the room with her as soon as they delivered her."

"The doctors just wanted to make sure she was okay. It's a normal precaution with a preemie."

"I know. It's just different when it's your own baby, you know?"

She smiled, even though she didn't know. Not really. "I can imagine. Especially when you're not exactly sure what to expect."

"I know what I'm supposed to expect. But knowing and truly believing are two different things."

Yes, they were. Natália knew there could be nothing between her and Adam. But her mind was having a hard time getting her heart to co-operate.

On the day Adam had found out about his wife's cheating, he'd gotten so drunk that the bar had called Sebastian's cellphone. When they couldn't reach him, they'd called her.

Natália had been forced to go to the bar and plead with Adam to let her drive him home.

She'd somehow gotten him up to his apartment and into his bed, tugging off his shoes and his slacks. Unbuttoning his shirt and sliding it over his broad shoulders had made her swallow. She hadn't been able to stop her fingertips from trailing down his arms…over his biceps, until she'd held his hands in hers.

He'd shifted on the bed and wrapped his arm around her, pulling her down until she was lying against him. She'd stayed there for several minutes, absorbing the feel of him.

"I'm so sorry, Adam."

Bleary eyes had looked at her without really seeing. "She doesn't want my kids. Or me, I guess." Natália could barely make out the slurred words. His fingers had slid behind her head, drawing her closer until her lips were within inches of his. "But you will, won't you, *minha* Nata? You'll have my babies. Lots of them."

Her breath had caught in her chest in a horrible spasm, the physical pain sending her wrenching out of his arms and out of the room. She'd leaned against the wall in the hallway, her cheek pressed hard to the cold plaster surface, suddenly furious. Angry at Priscilla for hurting him. Angry with Adam for choosing his wife instead of her. And blindingly furious at fate for not allowing her to give Adam as many babies as he wanted.

"Natália, are you okay?"

She shook herself back to the present. "Yes, of course. Just thinking about all the fun things you and Carolina are going to do someday."

Her friend studied her for a moment. "Does it bother you that I had Marcos Junior and now another baby?"

"Oh, honey…" She shut her eyes and tried to banish the specter of the past. When she opened them again, she smiled. "I already told you. I have never been so happy for anyone in my life. You deserve this. Both you and Marcos do."

Maggie's hand slid into her own. "Thank you for being here for me."

"I wouldn't be anywhere else."

It would be okay. She and Adam were both under a lot of stress with their jobs, it had probably just gotten the better of both of them. But nothing was going to happen between them again. It was one thing to leave pretend lip prints on the man's cardboard board shorts at a baby shower. It was another thing entirely to have her real-life lips pressed against his real-life flesh.

"That means a lot." Maggie glanced up at the monitor where her blood pressure still hovered just a touch higher than it should. "Why can't Carolina be with me?"

"You already know the answer to that. They need to make sure she's stable and stays stable. And you need to get some rest so that your meds have a chance to kick in and make everything return to normal."

If only there were some meds that Natália could take to make everything return to normal. But there weren't. Only time could do that.

Marcos, who had been in the middle of a treatment meeting when he'd gotten the news about Maggie, popped in to say that he had to go finalize things. He promised to return as soon as he could. Maggie had told him to do what was best for his patient. The tenderness in the kiss he'd dropped on his wife's forehead made the backs of Nata's eyelids prick.

Her friend was so very blessed. Thankfully Maggie knew it. It had taken her and

Marcos some time to find their way, but the love the two of them had for each other was obvious to everyone around. They were lovers who had become friends. Too bad it didn't work the other way around. But it didn't. Not for her, anyway.

Maybe someday Natália would find a love like that. She just had to start looking in places that weren't so close to home—and which didn't include a certain hunky ortho-pedic surgeon.

For her sake. And everyone else's.

CHAPTER SEVEN

ADAM GLANCED DOWN the long conference table where the members of Mr. Moreira's treatment team had gathered to talk about timetables and who would be in charge of planning each segment of their patient's journey back to health. He wasn't exactly sure what he thought about Natália attending this particular meeting, but Sebastian wanted her here. She'd spoken with their patient on more than one occasion and since they had all agreed that she would help keep him motivated, Adam couldn't very well ask to have her taken off the team. Not without answering some very difficult questions.

Questions that could put him in an awkward situation to say the very least.

As if sensing his eyes were on her, Natália picked that very moment to glance over and catch him staring. Her brows went up, then her attention shifted to the current speaker: Sebastian, who was talking about the chemo regimen he hoped to begin this week. They'd gotten the okay from the insurance companies and, thanks to Natália, from the patient himself. The only thing left to do was set the exact date.

"So what does everyone think about next Wednesday for starting dose one of the methotrexate?"

The treatment regimen was the one most often used for this type of osteosarcoma.

"Sounds good," Adam said. "Standard protocol?"

"Yes, unless we're not getting the results we want. If that happens, we'll re-evaluate."

A hand went up from farther down the table. Natália was asking for the floor.

Sebastian nodded in her direction. "You have something to add?"

"I'm just curious as to what 'standard protocol' means in this case."

"It means that there is a narrow window, and we want to follow what has worked for the largest segment of patients."

"He's worried about being sick and not appearing himself to the people he loves. Especially his daughter. Since she's a nurse, he knows he won't be able to hide much from her."

Leave it to Natália to think of something other than objective facts. But it made sense. Her area of expertise wasn't as cut and dried as oncology and orthopedics were. On the rare occasions he'd ventured down into NICU, he'd witnessed her tenderly holding those babies as if she could love them back to health. And maybe she could. It didn't work that way in his specialty. Cuddling his patients wouldn't mend broken bones. It certainly wouldn't cure Mr. Moreira's osteosarcoma. Or could it? Hadn't Sebastian told him he had seen miraculous recoveries in patients who—according to every statistic—should be dead?

And the way Natália had coaxed their patient to give medicine a chance… She'd spoken from the heart and used her own experience to give the man a sense of hope. Without her, this treatment team probably wouldn't be meeting to discuss treatment at all, but rather issuing discharge papers.

His eyes caught hers again as Sebastian asked, "What exactly is he afraid of? Losing his hair?"

"He's afraid of not being seen as the man he perceives himself to be."

"He's not going to be that man. At least not for a while. But it's temporary. His daughter and those who know him can help by not treating him as if he's at death's door."

Natália stiffened in her seat for a second, and Adam could pretty much imagine what was going through her head. Her family—and Adam—had treated her exactly like that during most of her treatment. Sebastian was still overprotective of her even now. He'd seen that first-hand.

Had they been wrong?

Maybe, but they'd all just been kids at the time. They'd only wanted to help and had done so in the only way they'd known how. Sebastian had done his best to shield Natália from their parents' fights—at least from what his friend had shared and what Adam had witnessed on several occasions. It had made his friend hard and bitter in some ways.

Then again, so had Adam's divorce. It had made him cynical in ways he'd never imagined when he'd been young and in love.

Growing up as the only child of emotionally distant parents had made Adam crave companionship, needing something to ease the gnawing loneliness. He'd tried to combat that by jumping from girl to girl, with disastrous results. One of those girls had gotten pregnant and he later learned that she'd chosen to terminate the pregnancy. He'd never told anyone about it, but that event had impacted his life in ways he never could have imagined. And it still did.

When Priscilla told him she didn't want children after all, he'd felt that same helpless despair of finding out that the child he thought he was going to have would never come into this world.

He'd done what his parents had done when they'd been disappointed in him. He'd withdrawn emotionally. And Priscilla had gone elsewhere for companionship. Just like he had in making friends with Sebastian and Natália. He couldn't even blame her. Not really.

He remembered getting drunk afterwards. Vaguely remembered Natália helping him up the stairs. Undressing him. Thank God he hadn't been in any condition to do anything that night, because the scent of her hair had tickled his senses, getting into his head and lodging there long after he woke up the next morning.

He'd stayed away ever since. At least until recently.

He glanced at Sebastian, wondering if he'd seen his sister's reaction, but if he had, he'd hidden it well.

Sebastian's voice smacked him back to reality.

"I agree with you, Natália. Maybe someone should mention it to the daughter. Adam?"

"Um, no. I'm no psychologist. That sounds like an area better handled by another department."

This time Natália smiled. "I'm in complete agreement. On both counts. Maybe you should start inviting his daughter to some of these meetings and have a counselor available if she or Mr. Moreira needs to talk."

"That's a good idea. Thanks, Natália."

"I just know it might help for the family members to figure out how to deal with their emotions and fears. I don't know if his parents are still alive or not."

Sebastian studied her for a minute. "Again, thank you. I'll take it under advisement."

Something in his attitude had shifted between her first comment and her second, and Adam thought he knew what it was. Their parents was a sticky subject for both Natália and Sebastian. Neither of them spent a lot of time with their folks from what he'd seen over the years. The three of them—Adam, Natália and Sebastian—had spent a lot of holidays together. At least until he'd gotten married. Funny how they hadn't picked back up on that habit once his divorce had been finalized.

Maybe because of those blurred drunken memories.

And after what had happened between him and Natália a few days ago, he couldn't see her opening Christmas presents with him around a tree.

He'd tried to catch her alone several times, but she'd always been in a hurry to do something. He got it. She didn't want to discuss what had happened. But they needed to. Otherwise things were going to continue to fester.

As soon as this meeting was over, he was going to try to intercept her and ask her to go someplace where they could be alone.

Like another exam room?

Hell, no. He'd gotten into trouble twice by being alone with her in one of those. No, it needed to be a public place, where they didn't have to worry about being overheard by anyone they knew.

He thought he knew the perfect place. Now all he needed was for Natália to agree to go. And to keep Sebastian from seeing them head off together. The last thing he wanted was for an already complicated situation to become an unbearable mess.

Wasn't it already that?

No, not yet. But if it kept going at its current rate, it was going to arrive there any day.

Natália accepted the chilled *coco verde* from the vendor with a smiling "Thank you," waiting for the man to chop the top off a second coconut and push a straw through the opening. He then handed it to Adam. She took a sip, sighing as the slight sweetness of the liquid washed over her tongue. This park was one of her absolute favorite places to go. Had Adam remembered their trips here or was it just a coincidence that he'd suggested coming?

A large dog pulling his owner on a skateboard whizzed past them on the bike path. Nestled in the heart of the urban sprawl that was São Paulo, the Ibirapueira Park was a green oasis in a sea of concrete. She hadn't been here with Adam in years, although she and Maggie came here from time to time to get some exercise. At least before her friend had gotten pregnant a second time and could no longer run.

She knew what he wanted to talk about—had done her best to avoid coming here. Having a broken cellphone was great for avoiding awkward conversations. But Adam had been quietly insistent, and since Sebastian had still been in the conference room at the time, she hadn't dared refuse, afraid that she'd draw attention to them if she did. So here she was. And nothing had changed. She'd hoped as a few more days passed, her emotions would settle down and that things would go back to their normal state—the same advice she'd given Maggie right after Carolina had been born.

Evidently they hadn't. For her or for Adam. Although maybe he just wanted to make sure she hadn't gotten the wrong idea. If he even suggested it, she might jab him with her straw and…

And what? Run away? Like she had in that exam room?

Yeah, that had been really brave of her.

Well, running away hadn't worked. And sweeping it under the rug hadn't worked. What was left?

How about talking like rational human beings, the way Adam seemed ready to do?

Not that she had a choice. She stopped and thought again. Maybe she didn't have a choice, but couldn't she at least make sure this discussion happened on her terms rather than standing there waiting for the ax to fall?

So as soon as he had his drink and they'd started walking down the wide asphalt path, she took a deep breath. "So I'm here. What is it that you want?"

His eyes darkened for a second before they left hers and moved over the scenery before them. "I think you already know what I want to talk about."

"Probably, but what I'm not sure of is why."

"Excuse me?"

She plowed forward. "It happened. It was a mistake. It won't happen again. Am I getting warm?"

"You always did cut to the chase."

"I'm blunt, remember? I don't believe in wallowing in sentiment."

"And yet you worried about how a patient might feel as he loses his hair, as his vitality sinks to an all-time low."

Natália swallowed. He'd seen right through her—just like he always had. There had been times during her treatment when she'd used bravado to mask her vulnerabilities. It had seemed to work. Then Adam would come along and hold her hand. When she'd yank it away with a scowl, he'd simply hold out his open palm and wait. Without fail, Natália would place hers in it once again.

"That's different."

"Is it?"

"Come on, Adam. Exactly what do you want me to say? We had sex. I liked it. I think you liked it. But that doesn't mean things have to become all weird between us, or—"

"I liked it."

"What?"

"You said you *think* I liked it. I was simply agreeing with you."

She toyed with her straw, glaring at him. "Are you making fun of me?"

"No. But we can't just slap the truth down on a table without taking a scalpel to it. It doesn't work that way. We have to try to fix this thing. Because things *have* become weird."

"I know."

He gestured to a bench under a tree, waiting until she'd sat down before joining her. "We've known each other our whole lives. After my divorce, I—"

"Oh, God, don't even go there." This was what she'd been afraid of. Getting lectured on how he was never going to get married again so not to get any strange ideas. "If you think I'm expecting some kind of romantic proposal, you're worrying for nothing. You are the last person I see myself settling down with. You—you're like a brother to me."

Okay, so that was stretching the truth a little.

His mouth opened and he started to say something, before swearing loudly.

"Adam!"

"A *brother*? Is that what you said? Are you seriously going to put me in that box and close the lid on it? Because, honey, that box never existed. And even if it did, we blew the lid off it in that exam room."

A muscle pulsed in his jaw. He set his drink down on the bench next to him and leaned closer, his voice deadly soft. "Let me get this straight, Nata. When we were in that bathroom, and you squeezed and squeezed and squeezed until you got yourself off... Well, that was something you would have done with a brother. Maybe even Sebastian."

Okay, now he was angry, and she wasn't even sure why. "Of course not. That's disgusting."

"Hell, I'm not sure what we are to each other, but one thing I do know. There is nothing remotely brotherly about what I wanted to do to you in that room. About what I want to do right now. What I want to do every time I'm around you."

She sucked down a breath, not caring that it sounded like an asthmatic wheeze. "Y-you do?"

"Yes, which is why we are going to think this thing through, if it kills both of us. We need to figure out why we shouldn't keep having sex and then stick to that plan." He pressed his forehead to hers, fingers sliding over her cheek. "So what I need from you is one good reason why we shouldn't go back to my place and do it even better than last time."

Was that even possible?

Okay, that was neither here nor there. He was muddling up her head so she couldn't think straight. "Because it makes things weird."

"Too vague. Give me another reason." He scraped his cheek against hers, his voice lowering. "Because right now all I can think about is the way your scent is filling my head with crazy thoughts."

"W-we work together."

"No, we don't, Nata. We work at the same hospital. There's a difference. Try again. This time make it good."

He was right. Oh, Lord. When he was pressed up against her like this, all she wanted to do was straddle those lean hips and ask him to do all kinds of naughty things to her. Maybe there was no good reason to stay apart. Should they just throw caution to the wind and go back to his apartment?

But wouldn't that be compounding one mistake with another? And this one would be a whole lot more deliberate than their impulsive foray last week. They would have to get up from this bench, drive several miles back to his place, go up the elevator and then get to the good part. They would have time to think. To have second thoughts. To change their minds.

It would kill her if he did that, so rather than open the door to that possibility, she said the one thing that she knew would knock this train off its track.

"Sebastian." The word whispered from her lips in a shaky voice. "We can't…because of Sebastian."

If she had balled up her fist and let it fly as hard as she could against that square jaw of his, she doubted Adam could have looked any more appalled.

A sickly white line formed around his mouth and the muscle that had been jerking in his cheek went totally still.

He stood. "You're right. That's a great reason. I'll take you home." And without looking to see if she was following him, he tossed his coconut into a nearby trash receptacle and started walking.

Her stomach bubbled up with nausea, and suddenly she was afraid she had done something that couldn't be repaired. Something far worse than sleeping together had been. She couldn't let him leave like this.

Not without trying to wield that scalpel he'd spoken of. She threw her own drink away and hurried to catch up with him, grabbing at his arm and pulling him to a halt. "I'm sorry, Adam. I shouldn't have said that."

He gave a laugh that was devoid of humor. "Oh, yes, you should have. I asked you for a reason, and you gave it to me."

Did she really want to do this?

"No, it wasn't, because in the end, this has nothing to do with Sebastian."

"I'm not following."

"Take me back to your apartment, Adam, and I'll explain it to you."

He stared at her, brows together, a stormy look in his eyes as they raked across her face. "I don't think that's a good idea."

"Really? Because a few minutes ago you sure as hell did."

"That was before you found the single reason why we shouldn't."

"I know, and I'm sorry." She let go of his hand, sending her fingers trailing up his arm instead, until she reached his shoulder. "We shouldn't. I know it. You know it. We don't need to come up with plans or anything else. We just *know*."

She hesitated, trying to drum up the courage to actually proposition him. "But that doesn't mean I don't want to. Desperately. I want to go with you. Please."

For a tense second she thought he was going to turn her down flat. They stood there, neither one moving for what seemed like an eternity. Then, instead of spinning around and walking away again, Adam encircled her wrist and carried it to his mouth, his gaze never leaving her face. When his lips touched her skin, the chill from his drink sent a sharp pang through her. *Deus!* She wanted that mouth on her. On her wrist. On her breasts. Everywhere.

Right or wrong, she didn't care.

"You're sure?"

"Yes."

Still holding her hand, he headed toward the park's exit, towing her behind him with quick steps, and she knew she was going to get exactly what she wanted.

And it couldn't come soon enough.

His fingers itched to wander. But they couldn't. Not yet. Not in the car as he drove toward their destination. Instead, he placed his palm just above her knee, letting it skim upward until it rested midway to where he wanted to be. The pressure behind his zipper was insistent. Reckless. His hand squeezed her thigh, thumb scrubbing at what he already knew to be incredibly soft skin. Skin he intended to explore in depth. Only this time there would be a bed. And any number of surfaces that would work a whole lot better for what he had in mind than a tiny hospital bathroom. Although that had been pretty damn good.

But this was going to be…

His erection jerked at all the delicious possibilities. But first they had to make it back to his apartment alive.

And right now she was killing him, because her hand was tucked under his ass. It wasn't doing anything, but he knew it was there. It was torture. A very, very good kind of torture.

Just a few more minutes and they would arrive at their destination. He wasn't going to ask her again if she was sure. He trusted her to tell him if she wasn't.

Hell, he'd taken her to the park to tell her they shouldn't sleep with each other again, and what did he do? Proposition her the moment they were alone.

His hand slid a little further up, only to

have her fingers cover his. "Any more of that, and we won't make it back to your apartment."

"Worried about my driving?"

"No. Worried about making you finish what you started."

"I always finish what I start."

She laughed, her head leaning back against the headrest, eyes closing. "Right now you're in danger of finishing it—finishing me—before I'm ready."

"Last time I made you work for it. This time I intend to do all the work. You can just lie there and...enjoy."

"Oh, no. I enjoy taking an active role." The hand beneath his butt squeezed, almost sending him through the roof.

Natália had always been outspoken and bold, but the thought of that boldness carrying over to this area of her life made his mouth water.

"If that's the case, I'm the last person to try to put a stop to it."

She leaned over and nipped the side of his jaw. "Even if you tried to stop me, you wouldn't be able to."

"You think not? I could. With ease."

"I'd like to see you try."

Fifteen minutes later they were in his apartment and Natália was squirming on his bed. "No fair, Adam."

He leaned closer, sliding his lips over hers. "You never should have issued that challenge, *querida*."

"Untie me. Please." She pulled against the two belts that held her arms apart.

He eyed her for a moment. "Are you claustrophobic?"

"If I say yes will you let me go?"

"I think you just answered my question. So that would be a no."

Instead, he unbuttoned his shirt with quick fingers, letting the material fall open before lowering his hands to his waistband. "Another belt. Hmmm, where should I put it, I wonder?"

"In your closet," she said, glancing over at the closed door.

He unbuckled it and tugged. It slid free with a whisper of sound. Coiling it, he laid it beside one of her feet, a silent hint of what he'd like to do with it.

Natália squirmed again. "I want to touch you."

"You will." He unzipped his jeans, watching as her mouth parted, her tongue swiping across her lower lip. He smiled. "Not that kind of touch."

This time, she frowned. "You're taking all the fun out of it."

"Remind me to ask you how much fun you had tonight. Later."

He didn't take his pants off right away. Instead, he climbed on the bed, legs on either sides of her hips, ignoring the belt for now. Then he slowly undid the buttons on her shirt. He wouldn't need to take it off completely as long as he could slide it…like so. He peeled the edges apart until her torso was bared of everything except for her bra. "Look at that. It fastens in the front as well. Lucky me." He flicked the catch open with one finger.

He really was lucky. He had the most beautiful woman he'd ever laid eyes on in his bed, wriggling with need. For him.

His hands slid up and covered her breasts. Natália arched her back and moaned.

Hell, yes.

He pushed up her left sleeve, exposing her arm and that white line where a surgeon had replaced her bone with a metal rod. He leaned down and pressed his lips to it. That mark didn't define who she was, but it was beautiful because it meant that she was still here on this earth. That was enough to fascinate him. Dragging the tip of his tongue from the bottom edge all the way to the top of the scar, he couldn't seem to make himself move away from it, kissing it again and again.

"Adam…"

Thinking at first she wanted him to stop, he glanced at her face. She was looking back at him, not with the unease that he expected to see, but a heat that blew him away. He lifted her arm so she could see. "This drives me wild." He kissed it again. Softly. Tenderly.

This time she did try to tug it away from him. "I've never liked people looking at it."

"It's an inspiration. You are a walking poster child for limb-salvaging surgery." His thumb rubbed over the site. "But I like it because it's a part of you. What makes you unique. Special."

And she was special. And beautiful.

A weird feeling surged up inside him, catching him off guard. He forced himself to take several deep breaths to banish the sensation.

What the hell was going on here? He didn't

know, but it was his signal to get this show on the road. He fingered the waistband of her pants. "Ready for these to come off?"

"More than ready."

Getting back off the bed, he peeled the garment down her legs, folded it and put it on the nearby dresser. Then he ran his palms up her thighs, the way he'd wanted to in the car, until he reached the bottom edge of her panties. He didn't take them off right away, though. He gently ran his thumbs over the strip of cloth that covered her most private parts, finding heat and moisture there that set his world ablaze. "Damn. I want you so bad I ache."

"Then take me."

He swallowed and tried to will back the wall of need that was bearing down on him. But it was too heavy. Too overwhelming. Off came her panties.

He hadn't actually gotten to look at her the last time. That had to be why his desire suddenly seemed so much sharper, so much more impossible to deflect with random thoughts of sports or surgical procedures.

So much for tying her legs apart and slowly having his way with her. It was more like she was having her way with him. And nothing about it was slow.

He hadn't packed a condom. Hadn't dreamed they would end up here this afternoon, but Natália couldn't have children, right? He hadn't been with anyone without a condom since he'd found out about the pregnancy. Even during his marriage he'd always used protection. "I don't have anything with me."

She frowned for a second. "You don't need anything. Remember?"

Something about the way she said it almost made him pause, before he decided it was all in his head.

Stripping down the rest of the way, he stretched out on the bed and tried to enjoy each moment as it came rather than try to dissect it or make sense of it. She was here. That was all that mattered right now.

He nibbled her chin, her lips, not giving her time to really kiss him back, before he moved on to new territory—her jaw, her neck and lower. He licked a spot on her collarbone. He wanted to mark her.

Something small. Intimate.

Just between him and her. But she would

see it in the mirror over the coming days and remember exactly who had put it there.

He sucked the skin hard.

Natália's moan shot his libido through the roof. He released her, kissing a soothing pattern over the area.

There wasn't time to do everything he wanted. So he chose the big things, leaving subtlety for another time.

Another time?

Don't think about it.

Nuzzling the underside of her breast, his mouth made a quick trip up and over the top, including the nipple in his journey. He did the same for the other breast.

Her hips arched. "Adam. I'm waiting."

And he was going to make her wait a little longer. Just a little.

"Almost there, *querida.*"

He dipped a tongue into her belly button, drawing his nose along her abdomen until he reached the hard bone that marked the edge of the universe. To leap past it was to land in the place where dreams were made. Pure heaven. He didn't have to test to see if she was ready, his senses transmitted all he needed to know.

Moving back up and over, he braced

his elbows on the bed on either side of her breasts, legs on either side of hers. "Open for me."

They did a sinuous little dance, where he placed a knee between her thighs as she spread her legs wide. His other knee came down next to the first so that he was kneeling. Down where his hands could cup that gorgeous ass and lift it high, lining it up.

With a whispered, "Yes, do it," she braced her feet on the bed and held her pelvis in the air.

With a quick thrust he was inside, his groan of satisfaction almost lost as his senses began to implode. His hands went to her hips, holding them steady as he pumped, the push and pull on his flesh creating an agonizing spiral that started to lure him towards its center.

He needed to hurry. One of his thumbs slid down to find that sensitive part of her, tapping gently in time with his thrusts.

Air hissed from her lungs. Not quite a moan, more like a pressure release valve that took charge when things got to be too much. He knew exactly what she was feeling. He increased his rhythm, pulling almost all the way out before driving deeper. Harder.

Her eyes closed, neck arching back as he continued to thrust.

"Ooooohhhh… Adam!" His name rushed past her lips just as he felt her go off, strong contractions gripping tight and releasing. A second later he shot into space, his nerve endings sizzling as a chain reaction started deep inside him.

He bit back a curse. It was too soon. But too late. He climaxed, pumping every ounce of pleasure he possessed into her.

Eyes squeezed shut, he continued moving, drawing out the inevitable for as long as possible, knowing he would soon come back to earth.

When he finally slowed to a halt, he was breathing hard. But, hell, so was Natália. And it was the most beautiful sound he had ever heard.

And the scariest. Because not only had he done what he'd said he would never do again, in the hazy realm of satisfaction his brain was flashing him a quiet SOS that was slowly growing—just like last time. The message was clear. When could he get more of the same?

The answer that came back shook him to his core: as soon as humanly possible.

CHAPTER EIGHT

THEY HAD BREAKFAST TOGETHER, which was strange, since Natália had not planned on spending the night with Adam at all. But once he'd released her arms from their restraints they made love again, and she got her wish to touch him.

And she had, in every way possible. Afterward, she had been too satiated to move, so she'd let him draw her close, her front to his back as his breathing slowly grew deeper. He'd fallen asleep, just like that time she'd rescued him from the bar. Only this time he wasn't drunk or muttering incoherently. And he was very aware of her presence.

She'd lain there, absorbing every nuance of his skin, his musky scent, trapping it all in the deep crevices of her brain.

She swallowed. Her childhood infatuation had not gone away after all. It stuck its head out from beneath the rock where it had hidden for all these years. Only what emerged wasn't a girlhood crush. Not any more. It had morphed into something much bigger. Something that she wasn't sure she could handle.

Natália loved him.

Loved. Him.

He'd made love to her like he couldn't get enough. Was holding her now like she was something precious. Surely that meant he felt something in return, right? They weren't supposed to have done this again. And yet here they were.

Should she say something to him? Confess her feelings?

Only if he admitted it first, because to be wrong was to be…embarrassed. Horrified. Unable to face him ever again.

As it was, she hadn't been sure how she was going to face him again anyway. Only here they were, eating a meal together. One Adam had fixed for her. French toast with strawberry preserves and whipped cream. She licked some of the cream off her upper lip. Why hadn't she known about this stuff last night? They could have had a whole lot of fun…

Scratch that. They'd had a whole lot of fun without it.

She caught him staring at her mouth. "What?"

"Nothing." His jaw tensed, and he popped a bite of his own meal in his mouth, chewing with a rapidity that gave her pause. He seemed to be in a big hurry all of a sudden.

Oh, no! Was this that awkwardness she'd been so afraid of? Was he sorry they'd spent the night together?

Should she ask?

God, she was so confused. She had never been in a situation like this before. Not even with the one man she had dated. Maybe because that man had actually talked afterward. Adam seemed intent on staying quiet and it was driving her insane.

Maybe she should break the ice. "Are you okay?"

"Fine." This time he met her gaze. "You?"

"Fine."

Well, great. That told her a whole lot of nothing.

She tried again. "What's on your agenda for today?"

"I have meetings most of the day. One with your osteosarcoma patient."

"He's not my patient. He's your and Sebastian's patient. I'm just there to help."

"His first infusion is supposed to be today. I'm hoping it goes smoothly."

"Why?" She put her fork down. "Do you think it won't? Did he get the port put in?"

"No. Not yet. He wanted to wait. So we're going to do the first treatment as a normal IV." He set his own fork down and rubbed the back of his neck.

Something was bothering him.

"What is it?"

"He wasn't talking a whole lot during our last meeting. Even with the counselor present."

She nodded. "I know. I was there, remember? He's probably in shock. I remember once I realized I really did have cancer and that it wasn't going away, a wave of panic went through me. It took a couple of infusions to get through it. Did any more of his family come up?"

"Besides his daughter, you mean? No. His wife died of a heart attack a few years ago. Right after they celebrated their thirtieth wedding anniversary. I can't imagine being married that long."

His tone had a hard edge that made her frown. Was she just being paranoid?

"Why does it matter how long he was married? I didn't have a husband or even a boyfriend, and I made it through just fine." Fine was a relative term in this case, because she'd felt a kind of detachment at home that may have been born more out of self-preservation than anything. Her parents' marriage was not like she saw with Marcos and Maggie.

Not like she hoped to have someday with her husband.

As long as that person knew she could never have his children.

She swallowed, glancing at Adam from beneath her lashes, wondering what was going on in his head. She wasn't about to ask, though, and her fantasies of waking up to find him leaning over her, stroking her brow and murmuring tender words, had just gone up in smoke.

He hadn't been in bed at all when she'd woken up. He'd been out here in the kitchen, fixing breakfast. And since he had showered and was dressed for work, she had a feeling he wasn't going to stick around for very long. Natália's uneasiness grew, and suddenly she felt at a disadvantage, since she was wearing just the button-up shirt he'd tossed aside last night. She'd obviously not packed an overnight bag and her clothes from last night had somehow disappeared. She needed to ask where he'd put them, though, before he left.

"My...um...clothes?"

"Oh, hell, I almost forgot." He nodded in the direction of a door on the other side of the stainless-steel refrigerator. "I threw them in with some laundry I had. They should be almost dry by now."

He started to get up, but she held up a hand. "Don't worry about it. I can get them. And if you have to go, I can clean up the kitchen."

"You don't have to do that." He frowned. "I thought we'd ride in to work together."

She blinked back her surprise. "I thought you had to be there soon. You're all dressed."

"I have another hour before I'm scheduled. Just wanted to be up and showered by the time you woke up."

So he wouldn't have to talk to her while naked? That wasn't quite fair, since she'd evidently been lying in a tangle of sheets without a stitch of clothing on when he'd gotten up. Her face heated. Her hair had been a wreck when she'd padded into the bathroom after crawling off that huge bed of his. She'd had to wet down the huge cowlick of her bangs in order to get it to stay flat. She'd been so afraid he'd already left the apartment that she hadn't bothered showering, had just thrown on his shirt and come sailing down the hall.

"I guess I'd better go and get ready myself, then."

He stood, picking up his plate and stacking hers on top of it. "I'll lay your clothes in the bathroom once they're done. There's a shower curtain if you're worried about being seen."

Really? He'd pretty much seen all there was of her. The sleeves of his shirt fell down past her hands when she went to move. She rolled them up, shoving them higher to keep them from sliding back down.

He stopped where he was. "Why do you hide your scar?"

She realized she had pushed the left sleeve

up past her surgical scar. Since that was a whole long story that would make both of them late, she gave a shrug. "Just habit, I guess. Why?"

He looked like he might say something more, then gathered their utensils. "No reason. Just curious." He turned away and headed for the sink, throwing over his shoulder, "There's shampoo and everything in the bathroom and a new toothbrush and tube of toothpaste in the medicine cabinet."

For the women he brought here? As soon as she thought it, she shoved it out of her head. That was none of her business. Actually, it was, in this day and age, but she couldn't imagine Adam putting her at risk. She'd only said that about condoms because she knew pregnancy wasn't a possibility. He probably used them on a regular basis when he had sex with other women.

And there it was again. That sneaky thought that made her squirm. Especially since she'd realized she was head over heels in love with the man.

Was she really? Or was this just another round of infatuation?

As much as she might hope so, she somehow doubted it. She'd known this man for most of her life. What she felt right now was light years from that juvenile crush she'd once had.

She just had no idea what she was going to do about it.

If she ignored it long enough, it would eventually go away, right? Just like those other girlie feelings had.

Like the desire to have kids?

Not a good comparison.

And she remembered the days of those softer feelings. Every time he'd brought a date by their house in those days, she would cry into her pillow at night, sure she wasn't going to survive the heartbreak of yet another girlfriend. But she *had* survived. She'd survived time and time again.

And she would survive this as well.

It was no big deal. She got up from the breakfast bar and headed down the hallway toward the bathroom and the sanctuary of the shower.

There was a light at the end of this particular tunnel. She knew there was.

She just had to be patient and keep on going—until she finally found it and followed it to safety.

* * *

"Hey, Nata, it's me again. Can you either call me or come down to the infusion room? We have kind of a situation here."

It was the third voicemail he'd left in the last fifteen minutes. He'd also called the NICU desk and asked them to have her call him back.

This was ridiculous. Normally he would just say to hell with her. If she didn't want to talk to him after what had happened last night then that was her prerogative. But their friendship wasn't the only thing at stake. There was also—

His phone buzzed. Glancing at the read-out, he saw it was from the NICU unit. "Dr. Cordeiro here."

"Hey, it's Natália. Are you trying to get a hold of me?"

His mouth tightened. "Only a couple of times."

"Did you call my cell? It's broken, re-member? I haven't had a chance to have the screen fixed."

He'd totally forgotten about her phone. "Sorry. You should have let me take it in."

"Probably. Right now, though, I have a

twin set of preemies I'm trying to get settled in. What's so urgent?"

Adam wasn't the only one dealing with a life or death situation, evidently. "Anything I can help with? Besides your phone?"

"Do you have any experience with newborns?"

The dryness in her voice made him smile. "Only if they have broken bones."

"Actually, one of the twins has a broken clavicle."

He cringed. "Ouch. They normally heal on their own, though, right?"

"Yes, sorry. I wasn't being serious."

He should have realized that. "Are they okay?"

"They will be. I just wanted to monitor them for an hour or so before looking at my calls. So what's up? Why are you in the infusion room? Isn't that Sebastian's domain?"

Not really, since it was normally the nurses who tackled that particular task. Although there was normally a doctor in close proximity in case something went wrong during one of the chemo treatments.

"Yes, but this is a shared patient."

"Mr. Moreira?" Her answer came back

quickly enough to let him know that she'd already figured out why he was calling.

"Yes. He's having second thoughts about treatment. Again."

"As in about the internal—wait, the infusion room. He's thinking of not even having chemo? Has he decided to go for amputation instead?"

"No, he's thinking about going home. Pulling out. Taking his chances."

"Oh, no! He can't do that." The fervency in her voice didn't escape him. "Give me another half-hour to make sure the twins are okay and to round up another doctor to oversee their care, and then I'll be down. He won't leave before then, will he?"

"I wouldn't have called at all, except he's been asking for you."

"I thought we agreed that I would help with this case. Where's Sebastian?"

"It's his day off, and I'd rather you not go running to him about it right now."

"Afraid I might spill the beans about last night?"

"No." He tried to figure out exactly why he didn't want Natália to call her brother. Did he want to be the person who saved the day here? To impress her? No. Not when a patient's life was at stake. "I just want to see if I…if we can handle this on our own first. If people go running to Sebastian every time a patient was scared or wanted to leave, he would be at the hospital twenty-four seven. He needs some downtime as much as you or I."

"You're right, of course. Okay, keep him there and I'll be there as soon as I can."

The phone went dead before he could even say goodbye. Damn. He was not ready to face Natália again. Not yet. Last night had done a number on him in more ways than one. Instead of driving her home from the park, he'd practically held her prisoner in his bed.

Well, the belt thing had been more of a joke than anything, but then he'd pinned her against his body as he'd gone to sleep, something he had not planned on doing.

At first he'd dismissed it as being too tired to rouse himself enough to get up and take her home. But he could have just admitted that and then gone to sleep on his side of the bed while she went to sleep on the other side. His bed was certainly big enough to do that. But he'd wanted to touch her. To be skin to skin with nothing between them.

His thumb had brushed across her scar as they'd lain there in the dark, and a strange lethargy had stolen over him that had nothing to do with exhaustion. It had been an emotional stillness that wanted to freeze time and stay in that moment forever.

But he couldn't, and to think like that was to invite tragedy.

Natália was everything that was good and kind—and she always had been—while he…

He'd just been tired. That was all. By the next morning he'd figured out how to handle things. First he'd faced her on his own terms, with his clothes firmly attached to his body. Although seeing her in his shirt had almost undone everything. He'd almost dragged her back down that hallway and started things up all over again.

Her clothes had been in the dryer, exactly what had he expected her to come out dressed in?

Well, he'd kind of hoped her clothes would be dry by the time she woke up. He'd done his damnedest to make sure that happened. The next best thing had been to keep the breakfast bar between them and suggest she go shower as soon as she'd finished eating.

It worked. She'd trailed down the hall, that fine ass of hers swishing from side to side with each step. He'd actually come out from behind the counter, and then he'd gripped the edge of it with one hand and willed himself to let her go. Even when the sun had streamed through the window at the very end of the hall, rendering the shirt she wore almost invisible.

Okay, so that was then, and this was now. How was he going to handle this next encounter?

With a professionalism that he was going to drag up from somewhere in the depths of his black soul.

Once he'd located it.

Then he was going to concentrate on his patient's well-being and leave the emotional histrionics on the other side of the door.

Just as he started to head for the nurses' desk, the elevator doors opened and the woman herself appeared. That was a whole lot less than the half-hour she'd asked for. He glanced at his watch, irritated to discover he'd been standing there mooning after her for almost fifteen minutes.

He wasn't mooning. He was...*considering*. He met her halfway, motioning her to the side away from anyone who might be listening. Natália waited until he drew to a stop.

"Fill me in on what's going on." She paused. "I promised Maggie I'd be there to see her off a little later. She's supposed to be discharged sometime today."

"That was quick. She and the baby are doing okay, I take it."

"Yes, they're doing better than expected, thank God."

"Hopefully this won't take long, then." He ran through Mr. Moreira's list of concerns. "They're pretty much the same things he talked about when he initially came in."

"It's normal to be afraid before the first treatment. I was."

"Yes, but it's not normal for the patient to ask to leave before even attempting treatment, unless they know it's pretty much hopeless. His case isn't. He has a great chance for recovery, if he'll just see it through. Otherwise…"

Natália leaned against the wall and looked at him. "Is his daughter still here?"

"Yes, she's already tried to convince him to stay. He won't listen." He shook his head. "She was so upset she had to leave the room.

He's pretty torn up about it all—hates that she's been dragged into this at all."

"Even though she's a nurse, I'm sure he doesn't want her to see him when he's at his weakest. I understand that all too well."

He swallowed. Had Natália felt like that? "You were never weak, Nata. You were—and still are—one of the strongest people I know."

Her cheek dimpled, sending a ripple of something through him. "You're only saying that because I beat you at arm wrestling with my bionic arm."

"I let you win." Hell, he'd missed this light-hearted banter with her. Things hadn't been the same between them for the last couple of weeks.

"Ha. Easy to say after the fact." She nudged him with her shoulder and then tilted her head and smiled at him. "This is good, isn't it?"

He wasn't sure if she was talking about their joking together or if she was hinting about wanting things to continue. And he actually didn't care. Because right now... it *was* good. "Yes." He leaned down to kiss her cheek.

"Were you serious about knowing someone who could fix my phone screen? I'm worried about it not even turning on."

"Yep, I have a friend who works in the IT department here at the hospital and does repairs on the side. I can run it down there, if you want. I can at least see what he says."

"Would you mind? My day is crammed with patients and I don't know when I'll be able to get downtown to the store." She reached in her pocket and handed it to him.

"You got it. Do you have a landline at home?"

"Yes." She scribbled down the number for him.

"I'll let you know what he says."

"Thanks, Adam. I really appreciate it." She smiled at him once again and said, "Okay, let me go see our patient."

When he started to walk with her she shook her head. "Alone. I think it'll be better that way. I don't want him to feel like we're an attack team coming to badger him into something he truly doesn't want. And if he really doesn't, Adam, we'll have to respect his wishes. We can't force anyone to get better if that person fights us every step of the way."

He wasn't sure he agreed with her on that

account. If Natália developed cancer in the future due to the immunosuppressant action of the chemo, and she tried to refuse treatment, Adam would fight her tooth and nail.

"We'll have to agree to disagree on that subject."

She frowned for a second at him before turning away and heading into the infusion room, following closely behind another patient.

He knew she wanted him to stay out, but he couldn't prevent himself from walking over to the glass rectangle in the door and peering through it as she went over to sit beside their patient. Mr. Moreira was no longer in one of the infusion "recliners", as Adam liked to call them. Instead he was sitting in the corner in one of the visitor's chairs.

He watched as Natália talked to him over the next several minutes, motioning to her own arm at one point. He had no idea what she was saying, but her face was serious. Mr. Moreira had yet to say anything, but he nodded or shook his head a couple of times in response to whatever she said to him. Glancing up, her eyes met his in the window, and she gave a slight frown as if worried that he might come bursting through that door.

Adam stepped aside to let another patient through, a young man who couldn't have been older than thirty, his head covered in a black beanie cap. His eyebrows and lashes were long gone, and he was paler and thinner than he probably used to be. But the second he moved into the room several patients gave him a wave, and he sat down, seemingly not bothered at all as they pushed a needle into the PICC line in his chest to start whatever infusion the doctors had ordered.

He then lay back in the recliner, chatting and laughing with those around him. The times that Adam had been down to this room, he'd always been surprised by the strength and determination on display here. Patients got to know each other, encouraged each other, cheered over successes and mourned together over terrible losses. But through it all most of them never lost hope.

When he glanced back over at Natália and Mr. Moreira, she had him on his feet and had coaxed him over to speak with the newcomer. She soon had him seated on the recliner next to the man. Their backs were to him, but it was obvious that the other patient was sharing his story. Natália knelt beside him, not worrying about pulling a chair over. In another five minutes, one of the nurses had appeared beside Mr. Moreira and he let her hook up an IV and tape it to his forearm.

A wave of pride mixed with something else surged through him. She had done what he hadn't been able to. What Sebastian hadn't been able to.

Because she had lived through what this man would soon be facing.

"Are they having any luck with Papai?"

He started at the feminine voice that had sounded from beside him. When he glanced over, Adam found Mr. Moreira's daughter, Sara, standing next to him. Tall and slender with intelligent eyes and a compassionate smile, he imagined she must look a lot like her late mother.

"Yes, I think so." He moved over to let her look through the window.

"*Graças a Deus.* He was dead set against this an hour ago."

Yes, he had been. But he also knew that Natália was hard to shake off once she'd put her mind to something.

Like making love to him?

Oh, he may have felt in charge that last

time, but she could have said the word and he would have stopped in his tracks.

Sara murmured, "I don't believe it."

Adam did. And in that moment he knew why his stomach had been in knots for the last couple of weeks and why his heart started racing every time he saw Natália. He was in love with her.

Not like the love he'd had for his ex. That had been passion and not much else. He'd known Natália, on the other hand, his entire life. He knew her character. Knew her likes and dislikes. Knew some of her fears. And he knew her strength of character.

Well, hell. He should have recognized it long before now. And maybe he had in some deep pocket of his being. But he'd also been too busy seeing her as someone to be protected and cared for. Not a woman to be reckoned with.

A woman who could somehow convince a patient to try, when no one else could reach him. Natália was a living, breathing miracle.

So what did he do about it?

He wasn't sure she even felt the same way about him.

And if she did? Did he even deserve her? He'd done some awful things in his life. Had played free and easy with love and sex and ended up changing someone's life forever. Did that mean love wasn't in the cards for him?

He didn't know. But one thing he did know. He needed to decide one way or the other.

Soon. Before it was too late, and the chance was gone forever.

CHAPTER NINE

"I DON'T KNOW what you mean." Natália cuddled her friend's baby close to her chest and stared into the elfin face, trying to avoid looking Maggie in the eye.

"A couple of weeks ago you told me that you kissed Adam Cordeiro, and now you suddenly don't want to talk about him?" She paused. "He's a good man, honey. I don't want to see him or you get hurt."

"You sound like Sebastian. I've already gotten a lecture from him. He came by my apartment late last night looking for me, since he couldn't get a hold of me on my cellphone, and I wasn't home to answer my landline."

"He didn't leave you a voicemail?"

Natália wrinkled her nose. "He said he left seven of them actually. But since my cellphone was broken, I never saw any of the missed calls."

"It's a wonder he didn't send the police after you. Marcos says Sebastian has always been a little over the top."

"A little?"

Maggie wormed her way into a pair of yoga pants. "Ugh. I swore I would never wear a pair of these in public, but since I don't have anything else that will fit right now, I don't have a choice. What happened to your phone anyway? I wondered why I couldn't get a hold of you."

"It fell out of my pocket at the baby shower when my lips were on Adam's… I mean, when I…" She stared down at the baby sleeping in her arms.

"I see." Her friend's voice held a wealth of meaning. "From the color of your face, I take it that your lips have really been in some of those other places."

"You can't tell my brother. He would go ballistic."

Was it really because of Sebastian's "over the top" attitude, as Maggie had put it? Or was she just afraid to face up to what was happening between her and Adam?

Maggie's brows went up as she reached

for her blouse and buttoned it up her front. "I don't know anything *to* tell him. You're being awfully secretive about all of this."

"Only because I don't know what 'this' is yet. I mean I care about him, but it's been crazy lately."

"Did you sleep with him?"

The blunt words said in Maggie's cute American accent took her aback. She wasn't used to her friend being so direct. That was *her* realm. "Yes. But no one knows but you. And I'd rather they didn't. Not until I figure out where all of this is leading."

Maggie came over and hugged her from the side, laying her head on her shoulder for a second or two. "I'm sorry. I haven't been much of a friend or I would have realized something was going on long before now."

"It's okay, it hasn't been 'going on' for very long." She forced a smile and jiggled the newborn, who had started grunting. "Besides, you've been a little busy with things of your own."

Marcos had gone to install the baby seat in the car and was then supposed to return to pick them up. Marcos Junior was being cared for by another friend.

"We need to set a date for you to come

over and talk, when my hubby isn't around to overhear us."

"There's nothing to talk about. At least not yet. I think Adam and I are still trying to figure out where to go from here. I don't want to keep falling in bed with him if nothing is going to come of it."

"Did Sebastian ask you where you'd been the night he tried to call you?"

"Yes."

"And what did you tell him?"

Natália bit her lip for a second. "I told him I spent the night at a friend's house. It wasn't really a lie. Adam and I are friends."

Or were they? Nothing had been quite the same. Although he'd seemed a little more at ease when she'd met him at the infusion room. They'd actually joked like they used to. And he was supposed to either call her with news about her phone or if she was really lucky and his friend was able to fix it right then and there, he was going to drop it off at her apartment a little later. Already her belly was sending up signals that his wanting to stop by had to be a good thing. Otherwise he would have just said he'd give it to her tomorrow at work.

Did that mean he wanted to be with her again? Or was he just being nice?

"A little more than friends, from the sound of it." Maggie frowned and stuffed the rest of the baby's things into a new-looking diaper bag. It was huge. She tried not to think that she would never carry a bag like that. Or that she and Adam couldn't ever...

Did he still want biological kids with whomever he chose to love? Or had his drunken statement been just that? Ramblings that meant nothing?

Maybe she should figure out a way to get a subtle question in about it. He knew she couldn't have kids, and yet he'd slept with her anyway. That had to mean something. Right?

"Yes, a little more than friends. But whether or not we should be together isn't something I've thought about."

"Well, maybe you should start thinking about it. Does he care about you?"

"Yes, of course." She stopped and made a sound. "I know he cares about me as someone he's known for a long time, but as far as relationships go...I don't know."

"I don't think Adam is the type of man

who would just jump into bed with someone that he—"

Marcos opened the door, holding a baby carrier. "All done, *meu amor*." He glanced from one to the other. "Did I interrupt something?"

Natália realized her face was red hot. But at least he hadn't heard his wife talking about Adam jumping into bed with her. "No, I was just enjoying cuddling this little one. Carolina is a sweetheart, like her mother."

Smiling, Marcos went over and put his arm around his wife's shoulders. "She definitely doesn't get her good looks from me."

Was he kidding? Both Marcos and his brother Lucas were drop-dead gorgeous. Then again so was Adam.

She swallowed, looking at the pair across from her. They were so in love, even after four years of marriage. Would she ever find that with someone? She rubbed the sleeve of her left arm against her hip, making sure it was still pulled down over her elbow. Smiling, she moved toward the couple holding out the baby. "I'm sure you guys want to get her home to her big brother."

Marcos set the carrier down and took the newborn from her. "I want to get Maggie home and let her get some rest. She's had a difficult couple of days."

"Stop fussing. I'm fine." Maggie started to reach for the carrier and gasped, slowly straightening. "Okay, maybe my C-section has left me a little sore."

Her husband let out a couple of choice words, making Maggie giggle. "Watch it. We have little ears now. Although I think it's kind of sexy to hear you cuss in Portuguese."

With a snort of what sounded like exasperation, he squatted down and carefully laid the baby in the carrier, fumbling with the buckles for a second until he finally figured out how to get her secured.

"Mmm…a man with a baby is even sexier."

Another pang went through Natália's tummy. Adam would look wonderful holding their child. Tears pricked her eyes unexpectedly and she had to turn away for a second while the pair threw a couple more quips back and forth.

By the time she composed herself and faced them again, Maggie sent her a soft smile. "I think he cares. You just have to figure out if this is what you want."

Maggie was right. She could stand around

wishing for children and second-guessing things for an eternity. But in the end she had to decide if she and Adam had a shot at happiness. And if they did…

She needed to have the courage to confront him and see if he could live without having biological kids.

And if he couldn't? Well, she'd been down some difficult paths and learned that she was strong enough to withstand quite a bit.

But a broken heart? Was she strong enough to withstand that?

She had no idea. But there was only one way to find out. And like Mr. Moreira, she had to make a decision—or maybe she should start asking for a sign. And then be willing to accept the consequences. No matter what they were.

Adam paused outside Natália's condominium and drummed up the courage to ring the bell. She already knew he was on his way, because the doorman at the complex had alerted her to his presence and buzzed him into the lobby. But that didn't make it any easier to push that button.

He had her newly repaired cellphone with him. Once his friend in the IT department had powered it up, the man had given a quick whistle. "Your lady friend is one popular woman."

Adam could have corrected him on the "lady friend" terminology, but it was more trouble than it was worth. Besides, he wasn't entirely sure that the shoe didn't fit. It was part of the reason he'd decided to drop off her phone in person, rather than simply hand it back to her at work.

"Why do you say that?"

"The same man has called her like a bazillion times."

A chill went over him. Natália couldn't be involved with someone. She would have told him, right? Wouldn't have slept with him if she had a boyfriend.

Yes, of course she would have told him. This was Natália he was talking about. Not his ex-wife. Or even him, in his younger years.

It was none of his business who had called her, but he couldn't stop himself from looking when his friend held the phone up for him to see.

The name Bastian with the number twenty-three in parentheses made him sag in relief. It was what Natália often called her brother. He swallowed. And if some other man had called her that many times?

Hell, he didn't know what he would do.

It was then that he knew he had to get this matter settled once and for all. Either they were going to dive in and take a chance on each other or they were going to go their separate ways. Which was why he was standing here on her doorstep, finger poised over her doorbell.

It also meant he had to tell her the truth about his past. Not an easy thing to contemplate, much less do.

Taking another quick breath, he pressed the buzzer, hearing it ring out loud and clear from inside her place. He expected her to yank open the door right away. Instead, the seconds ticked away. Five. Ten. Twenty. Thirty.

Finally she appeared in the doorway in a white gauzy top and slim-fitting black jeans. Her bare feet stood in stark contrast to the dark wood floor.

He didn't think he'd ever seen her so casual. Not in a long time, anyway. Well, she'd come out of his bedroom dressed in just his shirt, but that was different. She'd had on regular business clothes before he'd taken them off her.

Those pale feet fascinated him. Picturing her padding around like that inside of her apartment made him want to know what else she did in the privacy of her own home.

"May I come in?"

"Oh, yes. Of course." She stepped aside to let him enter. "Sorry."

"I brought your phone. The IT guy was able to fix it." Did he tell her about her brother trying to call her repeatedly? Somehow that seemed a little bit like snooping now that he was standing in front of her. He decided to just omit that bit of information. If his friend hadn't said something, he wouldn't have looked at the screen or tried to figure out who had called her. His ex-wife's infidelity had evidently sown a seed of distrust that carried further than he'd thought. So he pulled it from his pocket and handed it over. "He said it's almost dead, though."

"Oh, okay, I'll plug it into the charger." She went off down the hallway, calling over her shoulder, "What do I owe him for fixing it?"

"Don't worry about it."

She came back a few moments later. "Did you pay him anything?"

He frowned. "I said don't worry about it."

"I want to reimburse you. It's not right for you to pay for it."

"Can we talk about something else for a minute?"

She stopped. Looked up at him. "What is it? Mr. Moreira?"

"No, this has nothing to do with him." He shoved his hands into his pockets. "It has to do with us. Or me, that is."

"Us?" A wary look came over her face. Not a promising sign. Maybe this was a bad idea.

Screw that. He had to get it out in the open. Rip it off like an adhesive bandage. Otherwise the unfinished business would hang over his head.

"First of all, I care about you, Nata. I would never purposely do anything to hurt you. You know that, right?"

"Oh, God." She turned away and headed toward the sofa—dropped onto it. "Here it comes."

Hell, this was definitely not the way this scene had played out in his head. Still, he had to follow it all the way to the end. He went and stood over her. "What is that supposed to mean?"

"If this is where you give me the brush-off, you can save it. I'm a big girl. I can play big-girl games as well as the next woman."

Exactly what kind of games was she talking about? The kind that Priscilla had played? The chill that had gone through him before crawled back down his spine with an ominous slither. "You're going to have to enlighten me, since I'm not a woman."

"I mean I can sleep with a man without it necessarily ending in marriage—or even a relationship. Have a fling here. Have a fling there."

He'd done the same thing once upon a time, but hearing it come out of Nata's mouth made...

"Have a fling here. Have a fling there." He repeated the words, counting to ten as he did. A muscle in his jaw kept time with the numbers as they slid by. "Is that what we're having, Nata? A fling?"

"Isn't it?"

Her tongue inched out to moisten her lips, and a weird buzzing started up in his head. Heaven help him if it didn't bring with it all kinds of thoughts that were better off left where they were.

A fling. Seriously? None of the flings he'd ever indulged in had ended up with him holding a woman deep into the night. Or caring about what she thought or felt.

But one of them had ended with a pregnancy.

Somehow that thought made him really angry. He'd come here to confess his sins, and she was worried about how to label their relationship?

Maybe she was the one who needed to be enlightened. To understand exactly what a true fling looked like. "I don't know. Why don't we find out?"

He stripped his shirt over his head in one quick move, tossing it over the back of her couch.

"Adam? What are you doing?"

"Isn't this what you wanted? A fling here…a fling there? Or did I misunderstand?"

"Well…" She blinked a couple of times. "I guess I'm still not sure what we're talking about."

"We're talking about sex, in its simplest form. If that's what you want, I can give it to you. I've been there, sweetheart, more than once. I know exactly how the game is played." His fingers went to the button on his jeans.

She stood in a rush, her chin going up. "You think I can't engage in a little meaningless sex? I might surprise you."

"Then, *minha querida* Nata, surprise me." He reached out and gripped her arms, drawing her toward him, some of his anger giving away to baser emotions. His head came down and captured her mouth, body coming to life when her arms snaked tight around his neck, holding him with a fervor that matched his own.

There was no time for formalities. Or foreplay. He was already on fire.

Reaching down, he cupped her butt, bringing her hard against him. When he lifted her up onto his hips, her legs clung, back arching.

Hell, yes. This was what he was talking about. They could discuss relationships later. There was no way she could be this wild for him without it meaning something.

So he would just go with that.

In a small corner of his mind a warning sounded. He ignored it, thrusting his tongue past her lips and going in. She encircled him, sucking him deeper. Still supporting her, he carried her over to the wall beside her door and ground against her, wondering how to get his zipper opened and her pants down without letting go of her.

The warning sounded again.

He dismissed it, reaching again for the front of his jeans. Natália's arms suddenly left his neck and started frantically pushing against his chest.

Before he could fully register what was happening, the door to his right snapped open. Both of their heads cranked to the side.

Nossa Senhora do céu.

There stood Sebastian. He stared at them for a second as if not sure what he was seeing.

Then his hand landed on Adam's shoulder, yanking him backward, dumping Natália onto the floor with a thump. She'd just shouted her brother's name, only to have the hand on his shoulder shove him again. His heel caught on something and down he went, flat on his ass.

He was up in a flash, his fists going up in a defensive posture.

"Adam, no!" Natália scrambled to her feet and put her hand on his chest. "Don't."

"I trusted you." Sebastian stepped around her and from the cold words and the angry gleam in his eyes, Adam knew he was in deep trouble. And there was no explanation known to man that was going to stop it.

"How dare you come into my home without knocking?" Natália was shaking with anger and embarrassment. Worse, her brother was acting like a lunatic, stalking around the room throwing obscenities around like it was his everyday speech. It wasn't. Sebastian rarely cursed. Rarely showed any kind of emotion at all. A trill of fear went through her. Not for her own safety but for Adam's.

Her brother turned and fixed her with a look that could have frozen lava in its tracks. "I wouldn't have had to if you'd answered your damn cellphone."

"It was broken. I told you that."

"I just called the carrier and told them it was an emergency. They tried ringing it themselves and said it seemed to be working just fine."

"Wh-what was the emergency?"

"That I haven't been able to locate you

for two nights in a row. I was worried." He turned around and shot a look at Adam, who had buttoned his jeans and pulled his shirt back over his head. She couldn't believe this was happening!

"I was at work today. It isn't like I disappeared off the face of the planet. Why didn't the doorman call up?"

"He damned well did. You didn't answer that either."

Natália only heard the interphone go off right before Sebastian burst into the room—it was why she'd tried to push Adam away. Maybe it had rung before that, but she'd been a little busy at the time.

"I'm sorry."

Adam stepped forward. "You have nothing to be sorry for." He turned toward Sebastian. "You are way out of line, here. Your sister has a right to her privacy."

"You have a right to her privacy too, evidently."

"You need to dial it back a notch."

"Really?" Her brother's volume went up. "I come in and find my best friend—who is half-naked, by the way—doing his best to nail my sister to the wall, just like he's done with a thousand other girls. So tell me again why *I* need to dial it back a notch?"

The ugly image of that cardboard cutout with all of those lips stuck to it came to mind. Was her brother right? Was she just one more girl in a long line of girls? Maybe that's where this had come from…he was glad not to have to act any more. She'd been worried about whether or not he would care about her infertility when she should have been worried about something else entirely.

She'd asked for a sign. But, please, God, this wasn't the one she wanted.

She glanced at her brother, trying to make sense of things. "Sebastian, please. Please, don't do this."

Adam took another step forward, hands still rolled into fists, knuckles white. "Your sister is right. We are going to sit down and talk about this like civilized people, so I think you need to lower your voice before something…happens."

"Happens? As in you trying to take me down?"

"There won't be any trying involved." Unlike her brother's, Adam's voice was deadly quiet.

Natália's breathing, which had never quite

gone back to normal from Adam's kisses, began getting a familiar stuck-in-her-lungs sensation with the air she inhaled getting harder and harder to expel. The beginnings of a panic attack. Oh, no. Not now. The last time this happened had been back when…

When she'd overheard her dad say it would be better if she were gone.

She sucked down another painful breath and fought against the raging tide that was threatening to pull her under. Adam glowered at Sebastian, who was still throwing out angry words, but now they all ran together into an indistinguishable roar of sound.

Unless she acted quickly, they were both going to be witness to her horrible breakdown. She struggled to pull in enough air to do the deed.

"Stop it! Both of you! Just. Stop. It." She yelled the words at the top of her lungs.

Her world went silent for several long seconds, and she saw stars. Then she realized it wasn't because she was about to pass out but because both men were now staring at her, their faces tense—Sebastian's with concern and Adam's with… She couldn't tell. His eyes were dark emotionless pits.

Her own eyes stung with tears. She didn't

want her brother to be right. But his words were gaining traction in her head, replacing all the bright hopes she'd had an hour ago.

She stood straighter.

"I want you both to leave." Another breath wheezed into her lungs.

Her brother reached out a hand, but she lurched backward to avoid it. "No."

He tried again, his voice softening. "*Olha, querida*, I overreacted, and I'm—"

"Just stop." If he said anything else, she was going to burst into tears in front of both of them. "You need to go. I'm safe, as you can see. We'll t-talk about this later. But not now. I just want to be alone."

"Natália."

"I am warning you, Sebastian. I want you out of my house. Now."

"I'm sorry."

She didn't say a word, just went over and pulled her front door open. "I'll call you to-morrow."

Her brother's eyes closed, a muscle work-ing in his jaw. When his lids parted, there was a sadness in them that cut her to the core. "Don't hate me."

"Never."

He looked like he might say something

else, but then he turned and went out the door, pushing the button to call the elevator. He didn't look back at Adam to see why his friend wasn't following him out.

She actually had no idea why he was even still in her apartment. What did he think was going to happen now? That they were just going to take up where they left off?

Well, he was wrong. So very wrong. Unlike him, she had no clue how the game was played. But she'd obviously been living in a dream world where rainbows lined the skies and leprechauns waited at both ends, flipping coins to everyone who happened by. Reality wasn't like that at all. At least not for her.

Once the elevator swallowed Sebastian, she turned to Adam. And then, looking him in the eye, she took a shaky breath and pushed out the hardest words she had ever spoken.

"You were right, Adam. This was a fling. At least for me. I wasn't sure before, but I am now."

"What?"

She lifted a shoulder in a half-shrug. "Maybe I needed closure on an old childhood crush, I'm not sure." She pressed her palms flat against her legs to control their trembling. "If it helps any, you were as good as I painted in my fantasies. Thanks for explaining the difference to me. Let's see: sex in its simplest form, have I got that right?"

Adam's face had drained of all color, his jaw a ropy mass of muscle. "Something like that."

At least her breathing was back under control, even if everything else felt like it was spiraling away from her.

She stretched her lips sideways in what had to look more like a macabre death mask than anything resembling a smile. "I figured after what happened with your wife that you would be gun shy about relationships. I guess I was right."

There was silence for the stretch of a few seconds. Then he laughed, but there was no humor in the staccato burst of sound. "Yes, Nata, you were right. You were very, very right. Thank you for the wake-up call. And the booty call. It's been a while since I answered one of those."

Something about the way he said that planted a niggle of doubt in her head. She hesitated, hand still gripping the edge of the open door. "You said you came here to tell me something. What was it?"

She held her breath, hoping beyond hope that he was going to walk over to her and take her in her arms and tell her that she'd made a mistake—that they both had. That he loved her and didn't care that she couldn't have children. That he didn't need twenty women, or even ten—that he just needed her.

He stood there, staring at her for a long time. "It doesn't matter. Your brother was right. About me. About the way I was." He gave a half-shrug. "So, yeah, whatever...we had going on, it wouldn't work. Thanks for helping me see that."

Disappointment froze her in place. But she didn't have time to sit there and process his words, or even think about him having sex with the next faceless woman that came along. Because he was already tucking his shirt into his waistband with short jerky movements and scooping up his car keys and cellphone. Then he walked past her and into the foyer.

Her heart threatened to splinter into a thousand pieces. She turned to face him. "So that's it?"

"I think so." He wouldn't meet her eyes, simply pushed the button to call the elevator. When it finally arrived, he stepped in. Only then did he look at her. "I'm sorry, Nata. Truly sorry. For everything."

Then the doors slowly slid shut and took him out of sight...and out of her life.

CHAPTER TEN

NATÁLIA WENT THROUGH the next two weeks in a haze. Sebastian had called her at least a half dozen times the day after she'd ended things with Adam. She'd finally answered the phone and accepted his apology, but the words had felt heavy and wooden. She could tell he was worried about her, but there was nothing she could do about that. In time things would get better.

Hopefully he and Adam had made their peace, but she didn't dare ask, because even the thought of Adam was enough to send her spinning into a vat of misery. She couldn't eat. Could hardly sleep.

But she had to somehow climb up and get back to the business of living. She had gone her whole life without being in a relationship with Adam, so she could do it again. Somehow.

Thank God she'd never told him she loved him. That would have made this so much more unbearable.

More? Was that even possible? How could it be more unbearable than realizing that making love with him hadn't been merely as good as her fantasies? Those few hours with him had stripped the fantasies down to mere caricatures. The reality was flesh and bone...and love.

She would never get over him. She knew that for a fact. But she could still live a fulfilling life. She just had to figure out how to go about constructing that life.

Surely she could meet someone else. Be content with that person.

There was a tiny voice of doubt that rose up each time she allowed herself to think along those lines.

Forget it.

She went into the nursery in her unit and checked the babies and charts to make sure they were all okay. One by one she studied their tiny faces, some of them with ventilators breathing for them, others with oxygen tubes under their nostrils. All of them, though, had one thing in common. They were fighting for a life that would eventually take place outside a hospital bed. Just like she once had. And hopefully they too would find their place with people who loved them.

Speaking of fighting for life, maybe it was time to pay Mr. Moreira a visit, since neither Sebastian nor Adam had contacted her about the patient's progress. She checked the schedule she'd been given about his infusion times, then she drew a deep breath. He had one today, which meant he was probably down in the room right now.

Clocking out, she made her way to the oncology unit and peeked through the rectangle on the door. Sure enough, he was there in a recliner that faced her, his daughter seated next to him, holding his hand. He laughed at something she said.

She should leave. He looked like he was doing fine.

Just then his glance crossed her path and then returned to her with a frown.

Too late.

He waved her in. Oh, well. She plastered a smile on her face. She would just keep her troubles to herself. The last thing he needed was someone coming in and unpacking their sadness in front of him.

Sliding past the door, she walked over

and shook his proffered hand. "Just came to check to see how you're doing."

His daughter stood. "Do you want to sit with him for a while?"

"Oh, I don't want to intrude."

The young woman studied her for a minute then her father spoke up. "It's not intruding. Sara needs a break anyway, don't you? Why don't you go to the cafeteria and grab some coffee and a *coxinha*? Look out over the park for a half hour or so?"

"That sounds like a good idea." Sara turned and gave her a quick hug. "Thanks for all you did."

Dropping a kiss on her father's weathered cheek, she said, "I'll be back in a little while. Do you want anything?"

"I want a lot of things. Some of them out of my reach."

Natália could relate to that. The thing she wanted most was firmly out of reach, but she smiled as Mr. Moreira's daughter blew him another kiss as she went out the door.

"You're a very lucky man. Sara seems like a sweet woman."

He glanced at the IV bag next to him and sighed. "Yes, her mother and I couldn't have asked for a better daughter. She brought us much joy, especially since she was the only one we could have."

"Oh?" An ache went through the pit of her stomach. At least his wife had been able to have a baby.

"My wife almost bled out. They were able to revive her, but they had to take her...female parts to save her."

Normally she would have smiled at how some of the toughest men were unable to say certain words, but this hit too close to home. Natália's uterus hadn't been removed, but the eggs that her uterus would have housed and protected had been rendered useless by her chemo.

She decided to change the subject. "How long were you married?"

"Thirty years. She was our rock. I didn't think I was going to make it when she died."

Natália touched his arm. "I'm so sorry."

"Don't be. We had a lot of happy years together." He eyed her. "So, is this a social call? Or are you here to give me another pep talk?"

"I don't think you need one, do you? You look like you're doing fine. Any side effects from the chemo?"

"None that I can't handle."

She could well imagine the man could endure anything that came along. He'd survived his wife's death. The fact that she could only have one child. And now cancer. She touched her sleeve.

He nodded at her. "You're the reason I'm sitting in this chair."

At first she thought he was blaming her for something in the chemo treatments, then she realized he was talking about the fact that he'd stayed. "You have a lot of reasons for sitting in that chair, and the most obvious one just walked through that door a few minutes ago."

He gave a nod of agreement. "What about you? You have just the one brother?"

"Yep." Thank God for that. She didn't think she could handle another overbearing sibling.

"And that other doctor. He's your boyfriend?"

She swallowed. "Adam? No. He's just… a friend."

Not really. Not any more.

"But he was more."

She looked into his gray eyes and realized he saw a lot more than she'd given him credit for. "I thought so at one time. But…"

She gave a quick shrug, glancing around. No one was paying any attention to them. In fact, the infusion chair on the other side of her was empty.

"But?"

"Adam…" How did she explain it so that it didn't make him look like a jerk? "I…" She took a deep breath. "It's a long story."

"I'm going to be in this chair for a couple more hours, and if I know Sara, she won't come in until she knows we're done talking."

It would probably be unprofessional to talk about his doctor in front of him. "I don't think I should say anything."

He patted her hand. "I have learned over the years that there is no better listener than a steer. They don't talk back and they are very good at keeping secrets. The more I work with them, the more I value those two traits. I won't think any worse of your doctor friend. Or of you. You can tell me."

She did just that, words pouring out in short, jerky phrases. Some of them were things she'd never dreamed she would ever talk about. Especially not with a stranger. Her infertility. Her crush on Adam. Her cancer.

How she was so afraid no one would ever love her.

All through it, he listened without saying anything.

When she'd finished, he nodded. "My wife and I grew up in the same town. We knew the same people. We were childhood friends. We were so close that we never really looked twice at each other. Until I was an usher at a friend's wedding and had to escort her down the aisle." He smiled. "I remember she had on the prettiest purple dress, all lacy with these skinny little ties up the back. I had never seen her show that much skin. Ever. I was kind of tongue-tied. And then I looked down at her feet and saw the tips of her old beat-up boots peeking out from under the fancy dress."

He shifted in his seat. "Just like that, I was in love."

"That's beautiful."

"No, it wasn't. Not for a while." He cleared his throat. "I had never been interested in a serious relationship until that moment. And Isabela didn't want to believe that I could change. I had to convince her. It took three years of my life. But it was worth it. If I'd given up… Well, I wouldn't have the memories I do, or my sweet daughter."

"You were right to keep trying."

"Yes. I was." He shifted his shoulder where his port was. "When she had her heart attack, I kept hoping she'd make it. It couldn't be happening, not to my Isabela. And when she died…I buried her in those boots from that wedding thirty years earlier. She would have wanted that."

Natália dashed moisture from her cheeks. His love for his late wife was evident in every word he spoke.

"Not many people find that kind of love."

"I think they would, if they just took a closer look when the unexpected happens."

"Like what?"

"Like seeing cowboy boots under a formal dress." He smiled and patted her hand. "Like the unexpected passion in the kiss of a friend."

Like she and Adam had shared? But that was different.

Or was it?

"I don't think he wants a relationship with me. Not really."

He held up a finger. "You don't *think* he does. But do you know?"

She searched back through that last terrible conversation when Sebastian had accused him of treating her like one of the many girlfriends that he'd had over the years. Except she'd never really given him the opportunity to finish his sentence when he'd first walked in the door. She'd assumed, and then had gone on the attack. Just like the distinction Mr. Moreira had made, she'd "thought" she knew what he was going to say. But she hadn't known.

"No, but I think it's too late to do anything about it."

"It's never too late. It took me three years to convince my Isabela to be my wife. Surely you can at least spend a few days or a few weeks. Until you no longer 'think' but you 'know'."

Two weeks had already gone by, and she was still not sure what had happened between her and Adam after Sebastian had burst in on them. One minute they'd been kissing like there was no tomorrow and the next she'd thrown him out of her house. And like Mr. Moreira had said, she could hypothesize and rationalize all she wanted, but until she "knew" she would never be able to lay it to rest.

"What should I do?"

"What do you think you should do?"

"Talk to him?"

He glanced down at the simple gold band on his hand. "It's a very good starting place."

Natália leaned over and hugged him for several seconds, noticing that Sara was peeking in the door. She nodded at the woman, motioning her to come in. "I've taken up enough of your time. Can I come back again, though?"

"Yes." He gave her hand a squeeze. "Please do. I want to hear where your journey leads you."

"Thank you."

"You're welcome. Now go and find him. If he's as smart a guy as I think he is, you'll come back with some good news."

Natália didn't know about that, but what she did know was…she had to at least know. One way or the other.

Adam studied the fractured bone displayed on his computer screen for what seemed like the thousandth time. An open break, the little boy's collarbone had come through the skin after a bicycle accident. Every time his eyes traveled across the film, he remembered Natália telling him about the twins and how one of their clavicles had snapped during delivery. He'd told her at the time that there was nothing you could do for them, those breaks just had to heal on their own. That was normally the case, but here was concrete evidence that that wasn't always true. Sometimes they couldn't just spontaneously heal. They needed a little help from a surgeon.

What about what was broken inside him? Would it heal on its own?

If not, then he was kind of like the nursery rhyme, because there hadn't been a surgeon invented yet who could heal that kind of break.

He still wasn't sure what had happened. But Natália's words had found and gouged at every insecurity he carried around inside him.

Dammit! She'd as much as said she didn't love him. That she'd been putting her old childhood crush to bed. His lips twisted at the double meaning behind those words.

To hell with it. If she wanted to pretend there had been nothing more than lust between them, then let her. It wasn't like she'd given him much of a choice.

One of the nurses poked her head into the room. "Dr. Cordeiro? Someone is here to see you."

It had to be one of his patient's parents. He'd told them he'd be back with a decision in a few minutes. Time to get his act together and give them some answers. "Send them in."

"Them?"

"Whichever person it is."

The woman's brows went up. "Oh, okay." She withdrew from the room.

Adam stared at the break again. Okay, so he would have to open it up and give it a good wash with sterile solution to rinse away any grit from the road. Then fashion a plate to hold the ends of the bones together...

"Adam?"

He froze. He knew that voice, and it sure as hell wasn't the voice of either one of the boy's parents. Swallowing, he slowly turned around.

Natália stood there in her hospital gear, the pink scrubs sporting teddy bears and green frogs, a totally incongruous pair that somehow fit her to a T.

"Hey." His head spun through possible

reasons for her visit. "Mr. Moreira? Has something happened with him?"

"No, not really. I sat with him for a little while yesterday. He gave me some good advice."

"He did?"

"Yes." She came in and closed the door behind her. His teeth ground together. The last time they had been in one of these rooms alone, it hadn't ended well. Well, it had, but it had been the first in a progression of incidents that had finally come to a disastrous conclusion in her apartment. "Aren't you going to ask me why I'm here?"

"No."

Her eyes widened, and he thought for a moment she might turn around and leave. But then she sucked down a deep breath and came over to look at the computer screen where his patient's bone was on display. "Wow, what happened?"

"Bicycle accident. He was hit by a car."

"Oh, I'm sorry. You'll have to operate?"

"Yes." What was going on? Surely she hadn't just stopped by to discuss a random case. Maybe he'd just give her what she wanted. "Why are you here?"

She turned away from the screen and gave

him a stiff smile. "I'm glad you asked. I came to talk to you about our…fling. I think I know what happened, but I'm not absolutely sure. And until I am, I can't let it rest."

"Dammit, Nata. Haven't we already done this once? Do you think I didn't understand what you said?"

"No, I know you did." She licked her lips. "But I came to tell you that I was wrong. It wasn't a fling."

He inserted every ounce of sarcasm that he could into his voice. "No? What was it, then? A tryst? An affair? A…" he counted on his fingers "…two-and-a-half-night stand?"

She flinched and was silent for several seconds. "No."

Okay, he was lost. If she wasn't here to rub salt in his wound, what was she here for? "I give up. What was it, then?"

"I'm not sure. But what I do know is a fling is temporary. It has a beginning…and an end." She paused again. "I don't want the end."

His head was spinning, and a flash of hope went through it before he extinguished it again. "But it did end. So how is it anything else?"

"Did you love any of those women you slept with in your past?"

Oh, hell, no. He did not want to go there. But what choice did he have? "No. Not until Priscilla, and probably not even then. I don't understand what that has to do with anything, though."

"You came to my apartment to tell me something, and I cut you off. What was it?"

He searched his head for some cynical answer, but couldn't find one. He decided to go with the truth. Because once he did, she would be out of that room in a flash.

"I got a girl pregnant when I was in high school."

Her face registered shock and then something else. "You what?"

"Yep. Remember Sebastian saying that I slept with thousands of girls? Well, I didn't, but I slept with enough. And one of them became pregnant."

She blinked, and then dropped into a chair. "Do you know where the child is?"

"There is no child. She had an abortion. I didn't know about it until afterward."

"God, Adam, I had no idea. I'm so sorry."

"Yeah, me too. I can't imagine what that girl went through. What her parents went through. But it knocked some much-needed sense into me." He leaned against the wall, crossing his arms over his chest. "I never told anyone. Not even my parents."

"But you wanted to tell me that night. Why?"

"Because…" He couldn't bring himself to finish that sentence.

"You didn't love her."

"No."

"Do you still sleep around like you did back then? Like Sebastian implied back at my apartment."

"Nope."

She fingered her sleeve. "You know what I think? I think you have a scar, Adam, and you wanted to show it to me. Something you keep hidden from everyone. Just like the one I keep hidden."

"A scar?" He had no idea what she was talking about.

Then she said in a small voice, "Do you know why I cover up mine?"

"Because of what your dad said? Or reminders of what you went through?"

She rolled up her sleeve and looked at the puckered white mark where a surgeon had once sliced her arm open and performed a miracle. "No, it has nothing to do with either of those. This scar should make me happy. Should remind me of how lucky I am. But it doesn't."

"Are you afraid of the cancer coming back?"

She blinked, maybe thinking about her answer for a moment. "If I'm honest, yes, I am, and that's something that you need to consider as well."

"Because?"

"Because it might affect your answer."

"I didn't realize you'd asked a question."

"I'll get to that in a minute." She drew a finger down her scar and stared at it. "Do you know what I think of when I look at this?"

"No."

"I think of how it changed my life forever. How I can't have children. How my dreams of being a neurosurgeon will never become a reality. And, yes, I think about how my cancer might come back." She gave a soft laugh. "I used to lie in bed and wonder what I did to deserve what was happening to me."

He took her hand and tugged her sleeve back down. "You didn't do anything to deserve what happened to you. Whereas my

'scar', as you put it, was very much my fault."
His voice trailed away. "I'd always had trouble getting emotionally involved with people, and after I heard about the pregnancy it just made things worse. I couldn't bear the thought of hurting someone else. And when I finally did try to connect—with Priscilla— I found I still couldn't. Not really."

Not until Natália. And then he'd gone and wrecked that too.

She stood to her feet. "That brings me to my question. I showed you my scar because…" She hesitated for several long seconds. "Because I love you. Your answer to what I say next determines where we go from here. Why did you want to tell me about what happened all those years ago?"

His head went fuzzy for a second, sorting through the words and then rewinding them.

She loved him?

"Are you serious?"

Her brows went up. "Serious about which part?"

"About loving me." His heart leaped into a crazy rhythm, half-afraid he'd imagined the words.

"Oh, yes. I have for a long time, I think. I was just too afraid to tell you."

This time he didn't try to resist. He pulled her into his arms and held her as tight as he could, hoping this wasn't all in his imagination. "I wanted you to know my secret for the exact same reason. I love you, and I wanted to tell you what happened between us was never just about the sex. Not for me."

He kissed the top of her head. "When you started talking about flings, I saw red and wanted to give you a taste of the man I was back then. To show you there really was a difference. That I had changed."

Natália wrapped her arms around his waist and snuggled close. "Really? Because I kind of liked that taste."

"You did, huh? I'll have to file that little bit of information away and save it for a rainy day." His hand slid down her back, coming to rest on her hip.

"So what do we do if Sebastian never comes to terms with the fact that we love each other? I can't have him pulling me off my wife every time he sees us."

"Your…your *wife*?" She leaned back to look up at him.

He grinned. "I don't think Sebastian will accept anything less. And neither will I. Will you marry me?"

She placed a kiss in the center of his chin, her lips warm and lingering. "Oh, yes. I will. And as far as Sebastian goes, I've already had a long talk with him. I told him I love you and that that wasn't going to change."

"And what did he say?"

"Well, he didn't exactly give us his blessing, but he promised not to punch you the next time he sees you."

Adam fingered his jaw in mock fear. "No punching. That sounds promising."

"It's a start." She walked her fingers up his chest, sending a jolt of electricity through him. "I also told him he's never to barge into my house unannounced again, if he doesn't want to find us in a compromising position."

Adam choked back a laugh. "You told him what?"

"You heard me."

"Hmm...so there are going to be compromising positions in our future, are there?"

"Absolutely. Lots of them, in fact." Her fingers reached his chin then stroked along his jaw. "One of them involves being tied up with scarves."

"I think we've already lived out that particular fantasy."

"Uh-uh, I don't think so. Because in this

particular scenario, the person who is restrained isn't me. It's you."

A certain part of his body was beginning to like this topic of conversation. "Oh, it is, is it?"

"Yes. And you're begging me for mercy. Over and over."

He cupped her face and kissed her long and hard. "I'm asking for it now."

"Why is that?"

"Because I still have to meet with this boy's parents." He nodded at the computer screen where the image of a broken bone stared up at them. "And perform his surgery today. I'll be busy for the next several hours."

Natália smoothed back the hair from his forehead. "Don't worry. I can wait several hours. I can wait for an eternity, in fact. As long as I *know* that you'll be there at the end of that wait."

"Oh, I'll be there. You don't have to worry about that. Today. Tomorrow and forever. I love you, *querida*."

"My cancer could come back someday."

"That day isn't today." He smiled at her. "And if it does, we'll face it together."

"And children?"

"Don't you get enough of those in your line of work?"

Her fingers stopped stroking. "I do. But what about you?"

"I just want you, for now. We can worry about the rest when it comes along. There are a lot of kids who deserve a set of parents who will love them unconditionally. I think we could give that to one or two."

"Yes," she breathed.

"Let's go, then. I'll go talk to my patient's parents and get that little boy put back together. And then we'll go back to your place and, first and foremost, lock the door. And then we're going to delve a little deeper into that fantasy you mentioned."

"Hmm, I've been thinking. What's the difference between a fantasy and a dream?"

He stopped for a moment and looked down at her beautiful face as the answer came to him. "A fantasy is something that is never quite real. No matter how hard you reach for it, it evaporates. But a dream…" He smiled. "A dream can come true, if you're willing to work, and fight…and believe. You, Nata, are my dream."

"And you, you are mine. From now to all eternity."

EPILOGUE

NATA'S WHITE DRESS fluttered in the breeze as she stood behind the huge house in the Brazilian state of Rio Grande do Sul.

Right in the heart of *gaúcho* country.

It had taken a year from the time they'd professed their love for one another, but both she and Adam had felt waiting to get married was the right thing to do.

Sebastian had come around. Kind of. He was still oddly broody, but he'd seemed to realize that this was how it was going to be. He'd only said one threatening thing to Adam, and it had made her smile. He'd warned him not to hurt her or he would more than match that hurt.

It was a promise that would never come to fruition. Neither one of them would purposely hurt the other. She knew the man she was marrying. Really knew him. He was good and kind and stronger than anyone she'd ever known. And for the first time she wore a sleeveless dress, letting the world know that she was no longer afraid. She and Adam had broken down that barrier. Her parents were there, but Natália hadn't wanted the traditional giving-away element to be included in her ceremony. She wanted to stand on her own as Adam's equal. And he'd been all for it.

The rest of the wedding party gathered around her. All except for Adam, who would be there shortly.

Maggie had helped her with her hair and make-up and now sat with Marcos and their children in the front row, along with his brother Lucas and his family.

Then Adam emerged from the house along with Mr. Moreira, who had his daughter supporting him on one side and Adam helping him on the other. He'd gone all the way through his chemo treatments and had received his internal prosthesis a month ago. He was still regaining his mobility but was getting steadier and stronger as the days went on. Doctors predicted that he would be back to riding horses in another few months.

He'd insisted that the wedding take place

at his ranch, and since he'd been the one who'd given her the courage to talk to Adam, she owed him more than she could ever repay. He was going to be Adam's grooms-man, with Sebastian taking the role of best man.

Adam finally stood by her side after help-ing Mr. Moreira sit in a nearby chair. Se-bastian stood next to Sara, staring straight ahead as if not sure where to look. One of the ranch hands, who was also the chaplain for the large sprawling operation, waited in front of them, ready to begin.

Her left hand was soon enveloped in her husband's as the ceremony started, although it was kind of a moot point. Religious cere-monies were not binding as far as marriages went in Brazil. Instead, they'd stood before a justice of the peace a few weeks ago and taken care of the legalities. So really they were already married. She would have been just as happy to skip this part, but Adam had wanted to profess in front of God and wit-nesses that they belonged to each other. So here they were.

When they got to the exchanging of the rings, Adam took her hand and slid the slim gold band over her finger and repeated his vows. She did the same when it was her turn.

Then came the passing of the *tereré*, the longstanding *gaúcho* tradition that Natália had wanted incorporated into their ceremony. Mr. Moreira handed the ornately carved gourd with its silver trim to his daughter, who carried it up and handed it to Adam. He offered the first sip to Natália, holding the straw toward her and gazing into her eyes as she drank from it. Then she gave it to Adam. The cup went to Sebastian next and his eyes narrowed slightly as he held it so Sara could sip.

Then it was off moving from person to person, and Adam took advantage of the distraction and kissed her. Long and deep, until the guests' attention came back to them amid cheers and laughter.

The chaplain pronounced them husband and wife.

There was music and food, with most of the ranch joining in the festivities. Mr. Moreira had one of the bunkhouses—the smallest one on the property—scrubbed and decorated for them to spend the night in.

Their very own rustic honeymoon suite.

Natália couldn't wait to be alone with him.

And from the way he danced with her, arm snuggling her close as they swayed from side to side, he felt the same way. They would get there. When the moment was right.

It was that whole being willing to wait that Mr. Moreira had talked about. She knew now it wasn't the waiting that was important. It was the prize at the end of that wait that made everything worthwhile.

And this man—who rocked her nights with love and filled her days with happiness—was definitely a prize worth waiting for.

* * * * *